ADUA

A Novel

"UTTERLY SUBLIME."
—**Maaza Mengiste**,
author of *Beneath the Lion's Gaze*

Igiaba Scego

Translated by Jamie Richards

"Deeply and thoroughly researched ... also a captivating read: the novel is sweeping in its geographical and temporal scope, yet Scego nonetheless renders her complex protagonists richly and lovingly."

—*AFRICA IS A COUNTRY*

"This book depicts the soul and the body of a daughter and a father, illuminating words that are used every day and swiftly emptied of meaning: migrants, diaspora, refugees, separation, hope, humiliation, death."

—*PANORAMA*

ADUA

Igiaba Scego

Translated by
Jamie Richards

NEW VESSEL PRESS
NEW YORK

ADUA

 New Vessel Press

www.newvesselpress.com

First published in Italian in 2015 as *Adua*
Copyright © 2015 Igiaba Scego
This edition published in agreement with Piergiorgio Nicolazzini Literary Agency (PNLA)
Translation Copyright © 2017 Jamie Richards

Library of Congress Cataloging-in-Publication Data
Scego, Igiaba
[Adua. English]
Adua/ Igiaba Scego; translation by Jamie Richards
p. cm.
ISBN 9781939931450
Library of Congress Control Number 2016920555
Italy – Fiction

She's living the life just like a movie star.
—Santana, "Maria Maria"

Ah sacré papa.
Dis-moi où es-tu caché? Ça doit …
Faire aumoins mille fois que j'ai compté mes doigts.
Où t'es? Papaoutai?
—Stromae, "Papaoutai"

CONTENTS

ADUA

1

ADUA

I am Adua, daughter of Zoppe. Today I found the deed to Labo Dhegax, our house in Magalo, in southern Somalia. It was tucked away in an old pewter case I had in storage; it'd been there for ages and I'd never noticed.

Now I have my papers. Now if I want, I can go back to Somalia too.

I have a house, and most important, an official document stating in writing that it belonged to my father, Mohamed Ali Zoppe. Therefore, it's mine.

Finally I'll be able to clear out the squatters who've occupied it since those sad years of war.

Labo Dhegax means "two stones." A strange name for a house, perhaps not such an auspicious one. But I wouldn't dream of changing it now. It wouldn't make sense.

It started out with that name and with that name it is destined to exist.

Legend has it that my father, Mohamed Ali Zoppe, once said: "These are the two stones, the labo dhegax, upon which I will build my future."

Who knows whether he really said that? Sounds like something out of the Bible.

Fact is, by now the legend has taken root in our hearts, and I must say, regardless of its truth the family is still attached to it.

Every night before I fall asleep, I wonder if I too, like my father, will be able to build what future I have left in our land.

I asked Lul if she'd check on Labo Dhegax since she was leaving Rome soon.

I said: "Please, I'm counting on you, *abaayo*, to find out every little detail about my old house."

It was a windy day. Our scarves fluttered over the buildings of the capital.

I hugged her and said: "Don't forget Labo Dhegax. Don't forget me, sister." She didn't make any promises.

Lul was the first of my friends to go back. She called after a week in Mogadishu and said, "The air smells like onions." She didn't say much else. I asked her question after question. I wanted to know if our country had really changed that much and if those of us who'd been away for over thirty years could reconnect with the new, the brand-new, peacetime Somalia.

"Is our dream going to last?" I asked her. "Is it possible to make a home there?" I pressed.

But Lul didn't answer. On the phone she used words like "business," "money." She kept telling me that the time to make deals was today, not tomorrow. Now was the time to make money. Now was the time to cash in.

"That's peace, honey," she sneered. "If you care about

your two stones, come." Peace. Before August, I'd thought peace was a beautiful word.

No one ever told me that it's really an ambiguous one.

Civil war broke out in my country in 1991. In 2013, peace is breaking out. Hooray.

Now it's all about business for the Somalis. For Lul …

But I'm still in Rome and from here it all seems so strange. I love Rome in the summer, especially the light in the evening when the sun is setting. It's hot, even the seagulls seem nicer and make you want to hug them. They dominate the piazzas, but here you are, my little elephant, and they don't dare. Shoo, away from Piazza della Minerva! I feel safe when I'm around you. Here, I'm in Magalo—at home. My father had big ears too, but he was never good at listening, and I was never able to talk to him. It's different with you. That's why I'm grateful to Bernini for having made you. A little marble elephant holding up the smallest obelisk in the world. A toothpick. Don't take that the wrong way. I need you, you know.

Lul is gone and I don't know if I'll ever see her again. But you remind me of her. You're a good listener. I need to be heard, otherwise my words will fade away and be lost.

"Look at that black lady talking to herself," people say, pointing at us. But we don't pay them any attention. We understand each other perfectly, you and I. After all, we're both from the Indian Ocean. Our ocean of magic spells and scents, of separations and reunions. You're a nomad, like me.

Right now Lul is breathing in our tuna-scented ocean air. Drinking *shaah cadees*.

Ordering everyone around like *adoon*.

I know Lul, she's a good person, and for that very reason is the sneakiest sort of charmer.

Lul is first in my thoughts. What is my friend doing in Somalia now? What business has she gotten into?

What if I really went and joined her? My suitcase is ready. I never unpacked.

It's been ready since 1976. I should put the suitcase along with my tired body on a plane headed for Ankara and from there direct to Mogadishu.

But that's just a fantasy.

Yesterday there was this girl on the tram. She was black and had a shaved head and thick legs. We were on the fourteen where it turns toward Porta Maggiore. She'd been staring at me since Termini. I was irritated by her hard gaze. I felt like turning around and saying "Stop," like mixing my mother tongue with Dantean Italian and creating one of those scenes that make public transport in Rome entertaining. I wanted to be vulgar and go overboard. I wanted a big scene, that way I'd stop thinking about Lul, about Labo Dhegax, about the strange peace in Somalia. But the girl got wise. She sauntered over and virtually without warning shot me her question: "You're Adua, right? The actress? I saw your movie." And then after a pause, as if she'd planned it out, she added: "You really make an impression, you know that?"

I was completely rattled.

My movie? There was actually someone who still remembered that movie?

2
TALKING-TO

Don't misbehave, Adua. Get your elbows off the table. And wipe your dirty mouth. Sit up straight, for God's sake, why are you all hunched over? Your hands are filthy, go wash them or I'll thrash you. Is that how you look at Zoppe, your father, you heathen? You're just like your mother, Asha the Rash, that good-for-nothing. Your mother, that whore, who went and died on me, leaving me alone with nothing but my love. How could she let herself die? Tell me, how could she let that happen? That damn woman! And what about you? Are you going to die on me too? You have her eyes, I can't stand it! But you'll see, I'll fix you. There's no messing around with me, we have manners, girl. Now the tune has changed, it's not like out there in the bush where you were spoiled. And if you don't mind me, you know what'll happen, don't you? Good, then sit with your back straight and for heaven's sake don't whine like that, you're hurting my eardrums. Quiet now. That's it, be quiet!

3

ZOPPE

That February day in '34, pink dust covered the buildings of Rome.

There were three of them on top of him. One pinning him down, two pummeling him. The youngest gripped Zoppe with all his might. The brutes laughed with cheap zeal.

"Yeah, Beppe! Hold him, get that darkie bastard good." Beppe complied.

Zoppe could feel heat radiating from his skin. And he had soiled himself like a baby. *"Waan isku xaaray,"* he cursed himself. "Shit … why … me."

The words came out slowly. He felt humiliated, alone, a withered fruit on an unripe vine.

"Oh, Mama, when will this torture end?"

Meanwhile, blood had begun to trickle from his mouth.

"Mama …" he called.

Hooyooy macaan …

"This dumb nigger is talking to himself."

Hooyo …

"*Camerati*, this dummy's still yapping."

Hooyooy macaan …

"He really wants to piss us off."

Hooyo …

"Let's burn his feet, boys." *Hooyooy macaan* … "Let's poke out his eyes."

Hooyo …

"Let's break his nose."

Not his nose, not his beautiful nose. With a kick in the rear Zoppe found himself flat on the ground.

"You're disgusting, you know that, you little nigger?" Beppe taunted. "And now you want us to clean up your shit too, eh, boss man?"

"Come on," his buddy replied. "Lick it up."

"Party's over for you now, maggot," the three added in unison.

Zoppe saw the round toes of military boots over his head and squeezed his eyes shut. And he thought of the blond little girl and her giant father.

•

Zoppe was intoxicated with fear. But at that vision he trembled with joy.

The giant and his blond little girl. Oh, how he missed them. *Wallahi*, he missed them to pieces.

Seeing them in that strange dream haze was an unexpected surprise for him. Why had they come? Had they heard his cry for help?

"Xayaay, xayaay, xayaay, xayaay," he'd cried.

"Help," he whispered as they tortured him.

The father and his little girl …

They looked so nice together, strolling contentedly down the streets of Prati. For months he had seen them walking hand in hand. They lived a few buildings down from where he was staying. The first time they saw one another, it was inevitable: he studied them and they studied him. Without that vicious curiosity white people have, those ravenous hands in his curly hair, those vile comments about the color of his skin. The father and the girl looked at him with human eyes.

It was so nice to see them again in that dense fog. The vision had plenty of interference, but those two, the father and the girl, stood crystal clear against that sky laden with uncertainty.

He wanted to tell them, "Thank you for coming to see me in this dark hour," but can you say thank you to a vision? And his mouth was too swollen with blood to be usable. He could only sputter curses and prayers, in no particular order.

In other circumstances, he would have stood up and embraced them. Yet they remained shadows, projections, visions. They were neither made of flesh nor bone. They were there worried about him. Every vision, as his soothsayer father told him, always has some basis in truth, in the incarnate. The man and girl weren't really there, but maybe they were thinking about him. They had sensed, glimpsed something, in a mental haze.

Father and daughter didn't know he was in danger, but

sensitive souls can catch a scent in the air like warthogs. Nothing ever gets past them, at least according to his old man. Oh how wonderful it would have been to actually touch them, smother them with affection, melt into their kind concern. But Zoppe didn't know how to embrace people. In his village in Somalia, hugging was for the privacy of the marriage bed, the intimacy of lovers. An embrace wasn't something to spread around. Hugs weren't for friends or people you met.

Zoppe couldn't feel the brutal kicks anymore. All that existed were the father and the girl, hand in hand, on the hilly streets of Prati.

And then his mind drifted to his sister, Ayan … "I miss you …"

"Magalo is so far away, my little sister. Magalo is so far from this city I've ended up in. You must be grown now, you must be a woman. Tell me, Ayan, what are you doing? There, now, what are you doing?

Zoppe searched for her, but she wasn't there. "I wonder if our father taught you to read the stars," he thought.

He was thirsty. So, so thirsty.

•

"Let's give it a rest, eh boys?" Beppe said after a while.

"Yeah, otherwise we'll kill him. They told us to just have some fun with him. Not to kill him. He works for us, after all, and it's not like we have stockpiles of interpreters. My commander always says we ought to treat these ones with kid gloves; they'll be useful soon in the war against the dirty Abyssinians …"

"But if he's a nigger, what use is a nigger? Come on, man, be serious."

Zoppe barely heard their words. They could do whatever they wanted with him. His fate was already written. It was all *maktuub*.

He remembered his father telling him: "Look at the stars and then at their reflection in the basin. In that light, you will find yourself." How long had it been since he'd performed the rites? Rome had made him so lazy. He forgot to pray five times a day to Mecca, he forgot to bless his ancestors, he even forgot the simplest *duco*.

His father would have berated him and his sister, Ayan, would have looked down on him. They wouldn't listen to him and might not even believe his complaints. "There are no stars here in Rome, you can't see them, they blend in."

"The stars," his father would have said, "aren't in the sky. You haven't even tried to look for them."

It was true. He was consumed by work. Every day he had to translate, translate, translate, translate. There were words to decipher every minute, sighs to indicate every second, and all those damned commas to figure out. He was an interpreter, virtually a magician. It was a serious job, not like the *askari* who had to blow the bugle and trek across the sand, cannon fodder for the battlefield. He was always elegant in his khakis. Never an irksome wrinkle to ruin his symmetry. He was one of the best in the field.

Everyone told him he was the best. In a class of his own. Even a few party officials had noticed him. He spoke Arabic, Somali, Swahili, Amharic, Tigrinya, and several minor languages that would useful for the coming war. He had gotten this gift from his soothsayer father. Italian, on the other hand, came from the Jesuits. It had taken him some time to break it in and master it. He thought that working for the country's new masters would yield him a nest egg. "I wouldn't do that, my boy," his father said upon learning his intentions. "The stars say ..." But Zoppe interrupted him: "Enough with the stars, Father. Real life is about money, and I want enough to have a happy life and be the envy of everyone. I want people to kneel at my feet." His father looked at him the way one would look at excrement. But he said nothing. We each have our own path to follow, our own missteps to make. He fell silent and gave no more advice to that deranged son fate had brought him. Zoppe was satisfied with that silence. His father and all his wisdom got on his nerves. He was always so moral, so perfect. "Let me make my own mistakes in peace," Zoppe yelled once he was alone.

"You're not dead, are you, little nigger?" said Beppe, nudging him.

Before those blows and insults there was a time when he had felt fulfilled by that motley world that praised him, those people who complimented him. It was Rome itself that had conquered him. When he'd been told he would be going to spend a few months in Italy, in the Eternal City, Zoppe thought it was a miracle. A Negro in Rome? Him?

Rome was his dream, he knew it even before seeing it. "We'll give you some work. Mostly documents to translate." He accepted that transfer like a prize, recognition for his sacrifice, his loyalty. The work was plentiful, but most of all, painful. Because those papers stank of betrayal. War was nigh and some were already rushing into the victors' open arms. They could have said the same thing about him, even called him a collaborator. But he wasn't betraying anyone. He would never take arms against a neighbor, a man with the same color skin. He translated, that's all. He was a linguistic ambassador, a mediator, he didn't hurt anyone. His work involved the present, the passing moment. And maybe he would end up with a nice chunk of change. He would return to his land and build a big house one day. There he would bring Asha, daughter of old Said the Sightless, there he would take her, there she would become his woman, there she would raise their heirs.

•

The vision was still there, comforting him.

Father and daughter ... The streets ... The trees ... The dome of St. Peter's ... And the wisteria in bloom ... The women's perfume ... Take-away sorbet ... The soldiers' military step ... The rustle of colored skirts ... The cries of swaddled newborns … Boots on cracked stones … And another father … And another daughter … The touch of their hands … Their smiles …

Their hopes painted in the sky …

Zoppe was comforted by those murky, shaky images. By those visions, softer than the wind.

His photographic memory surprised him.

He had recorded every detail, every nuance of the recent past. He remembered the girl in particular.

Her little flower-print dress, tan coat, red gloves, and that felt bucket hat.

What a pretty little head she had. An oval-shaped head that disappeared entirely in that tiny old hat.

She reminded him of his sister, Ayan.

Ayan had a pretty head too. But Ayan never had a cute hat like that. "If I come out of this alive," he muttered, "I'll get her one just like it."

Fists had been replaced by feet. They kicked him good and hard. Zoppe clung to the vision so as not to give in to death.

They were shadows in front of him, but it was to them that he entrusted his soul. The girl smiled. Zoppe noticed tenderly that she was losing her baby teeth.

"If these goons ruin my nose, the little girl won't recognize me." The thought of his face changing terrified Zoppe.

"I hope your papa takes you away. As far away as possible. Yes … as far away from here as possible."

•

Zoppe remembered going for lunch at the man and his daughter's house three months earlier.

It was a Wednesday and there was an unusual air of anticipation in the streets.

The smells from the countryside formed a heady mix with the acrid scents of the city.

Horsehair, wild rose, and hay merged with automobile combustion and motor scooter exhaust.

"Why don't you come to our house for lunch?" the little girl asked him.

Zoppe, who was dressed in his usual khaki uniform, was taken aback by the odd invitation.

He was standing on the corner, ready to cross the street and rush toward his daily life, toward more words to translate. The little girl was standing on the same street corner.

And her giant father a few steps away, shielding her from wind and desperation. "Anyway my name's Emanuela, with an *E*, mind you. I don't like it when they call me Manuela with an *M*," and then taking a breath, she added, "and this is my papa. His name's Davide. Now shake hands. That's good, like friends."

And they shook hands. All three.

The little girl had a know-it-all tone. Almost annoying. She liked being bossy. You could tell that her parents spoiled her rotten, she was the darling of the house. She had no discipline.

But all the same there was something about her that delighted Zoppe. The Somali extended his right arm and opened his hand to greet Davide.

Zoppe noticed that he had a firm, powerful grip. A grip that put you at ease and gave you a sense of trustworthiness.

"So will you come?" the little girl implored.

He had been observing them from afar for a while. The father and his little girl. The little girl and her father.

Same keen eyes. Same furrowed brow. At a glance the girl seemed eight, maybe nine.

The same age as Ayan.

And she too had eyes that sparkled like emeralds in the sun. "So will you come?" the little girl asked. What could he say?

He had been in that strange land for months now and the girl with her big father were the only people who ever gave him a nod of greeting. The only ones in those nasty never-ending months. In that city that had been so stingy with him. And to think that he had imagined blonde girls at his beck and call and hordes of friends to play billiards with. But he had quickly discovered that a Negro in Rome had to keep vigilant. "If possible," one of his supervisors had told him, "you should do everything you can to disappear."

He had imagined Rome to be an open-air palace, but instead it was a pisspot for dogs and humans alike. And sometimes the latrine stench turned his stomach. But never as much as the sorrow of seeing how unliked he was. Sometimes others' disgust provoked unexpected gobs of spit that he'd learned to dodge with great skill.

That's why he was supposed to disappear, make himself invisible.

When he was out, he was always in a hurry. He wanted to be seen as an optical illusion, not a Negro.

Now he crossed Rome like a thunderbolt. No one noticed him anymore. He was too fast to catch.

He missed Magalo and the bovine slowness of that ocean city. There, he was important, at all hours of the day and night. No woman snubbed him or shunned him. He had all the women he wanted.

"My name's Emanuela, what's your name, mister?" the girl asked.

"My name is Mohamed Ali, but everyone calls me Zoppe."

"Zoppe because you're *zoppo*?" the girl asked.

"Yes, because of my limp. When I was little I caught a bad illness, but I was saved."

"He was lucky," Davide broke in.

"Lucky … it's true," Zoppe replied.

"Papa and I have been seeing you around for a while, you know?" the girl said.

"Well, I've seen you too," Zoppe wanted to tell them, but said nothing. He waited for the strange passing pair to continue.

"So will you come over? Huh? Will you come?"

"I don't know. I wasn't prepared to have lunch out," Zoppe replied, embarrassed.

"You don't have to be prepared, mister."

"Don't be rude, Emanuela," her father admonished.

"Don't worry," Zoppe cut in. "She's young. I spoke that way when I was little too. That's the nice thing about that age, don't you think?"

"When you were little were you brown like you are now?" she asked. The father went pale and reddened.

"Emanuela, don't make the gentleman uncomfortable."

"It's fine, really," replied Zoppe, amused. "I can answer your daughter. Yes, brown when I was little too. The same way you're pink, I was brown and I still am, as you see."

"Are there ferocious lions in your town? I saw them in books at school."

"Yes, and zebras too," Zoppe replied.

"And rhinoceroses? Have you seen rhinoceroses?"

"Yes, and more, there are antelopes, hyenas, giraffes, and one day I even saw a herd of wildebeests ready to chase a dream."

"What's a wildebeest? That's not in my book. What is it like?"

"It's like a big cow with a hump and lots of hair."

"Do you eat it?"

"I've never tried it."

The little girl looked at him in awe. Her father's eyes were filled with curiosity too. "This is the first time that a brown man is coming to eat with us. And you're lucky, today Mama made a big pot of artichokes and a cherry tart."

"Sounds good. But I don't have anything to bring you. Let me at least pick up some cookies."

"You're our guest today," said Davide. "Today you're sacred to us. Tomorrow you can get cookies if you like."

Zoppe smiled. He was no longer used to kindness.

"Well I'm curious too," he added. "I've never been in a Catholic home. Do you have a crucifix?"

The girl looked at her father.

Zoppe sensed that something in the cheerful atmosphere from before had broken. "We're different," the father murmured.

"The kids at school call me 'killer.' They say I killed God and my family goes around stealing children. Yesterday, Graziella, the fat one who still doesn't even know the alphabet, pulled my hair and called me 'pork-hater.' I started crying 'cause she pulled it so hard."

Zoppe didn't understand, confused by the rush of words. "Emanuela," the father broke in, "is trying to say that we're Jewish. Is that a problem for you?"

4

ADUA

My father has never seen my movie. If he has he never told me.

Haji Mohamed Ali, aka Zoppe, my father.

It's funny to feel the sound of that word in my mouth. When he was alive, I didn't call him Papa much. He was just Haji Mohamed. Haji because, like every believer worthy of the title, he too had made a pilgrimage to the Holy Land.

And anyway the truth, my little elephant, is that we never got along.

We both had strong personalities, we were prima donnas, battered by life. Neither made room for the other and sparks were inevitable.

Although by the end our relationship had become almost decent, in the beginning it was out-and-out war between us.

To me, my father was "the one who brought me into the world" or "the man who impregnated my mother" or "the person who tore me away from real life."

Never Papa.

But since I've been bombarding myself with questions, elephant, I've reclaimed this word. It has a bittersweet taste, the word "father." Its spines poke the tip of my tongue. But my palate is somehow soothed by it.

The word makes me uncomfortable. It's as if I have no support. As if it delegated my happiness to someone else. The word father terrifies me. But it's the only one that can help me breathe anymore.

I'm pretty rusty at saying it. I'm not used to its vibrations. I'm not used to all its deep curves. And what if using it too much pushes me into a hole, with no way out? Who will save me from myself then?

You, elephant, or what? Father …

Aabe …

I say it again. I've gotten a taste for it. Father …

Aabe …

I'm old, flabby. Maybe I can allow myself this difficult truth with you.

My husband, the boy I married, I never talk to him. I don't even know why we got married.

He was a Titanic, someone who'd risked drowning at sea to come here, a boater who landed at Lampedusa, a bum. He needed a house, a teat, a bowl of soup, a pillow, some money, hope, any semblance of relief. He needed a mama, a *hooyo*, a whore, a woman, a *sharmutta*, me. And even if I'm all wrinkled, I was able to give him what he was looking for. I didn't want a nice young man like him out starving on Via Giolitti.

I got him to toss that bottle of cheap gin that he bought from the Bengali and that kept him warm on cold Roman nights. I got him to toss it and took him in, here on Via Alberto da Giussano, in Pigneto.

There were not many guests at our wedding. I called a few friends, we ate *sanbuusi*.

Someone gave me a *shaash*, like a regular virgin bride. They perfumed me, massaged me, hennaed my hands.

I wore an old costume that had belonged to the famous actress with the gray eyes. I snatched it at Cinecittà during that fateful 1977. The cast was just steps away from my set, from my movie. I'm not a thief, but that dress felt like it was mine. It was a three-piece dress: bodice, capelet, petticoat. One of those old outfits that could have come out of the closet of a Jane Austen character. The ochre linen gave me a certain solemn air, which was promptly broken by the pearly violet flowers dotting the dress. But it was the taffeta petticoat that really gave me substance. That taffeta hidden from the world made me feel precious. I was a cloud. Frothy and free like the foam on a Guinness.

The women sang ritual songs for the new union. I laughed. It was nice to hear them. No one had ever sung for me. No one had ever celebrated me. It was a joy, a great joy.

And so I laughed, happy for all the tradition finally washing over me.

The wedding made no scandal among the Somalis of Rome. "You did the right thing, sister," several of the women told me. "You chose your little lamb well," they remarked, winking.

After all, I'm not the only one to do it, I wasn't the first.

There are lots of us now who have gotten a second youth with these fresh arrivals. No one sees anything wrong with it. It's a perfect trade. They get a roof and we get a little attention. They kiss us and we sew their holey socks.

One day they'll go away, toward love, other lands. But for now, they're curled up at our feet, ready to satisfy our longings.

Every night my little man falls asleep on my droopy chest like a baby hungry for milk. I rub his head and nestle my hand in his hair. It makes him forget the cruel waves of the Mediterranean that nearly swallowed him up. It makes him forget the tranquilizers they put in the bland soup at the immigrant welcome center. It makes him forget the girl he used to love, who was raped and murdered by Libyans in the desert.

He dozes off on my grandmotherly breast and gets an erection. So many times I've asked myself: "Don't I disgust him?" But he says: "You're so beautiful. No woman is as beautiful as you."

Only when he gets mad does he call me Old Lira. That's what young Titanics call women from the diaspora. They are as cruel to us as we are to them. It's not fair to call someone who risked their life at sea the name of a shipwreck. One time my husband even said to me: "I know that *Titanic* is a movie where everybody dies. But remember that I'm not dead." Old Lira, in comparison, is harmless. And maybe it's even true. When many of us came to this strange peninsula it wasn't the euro that captured our dreams, it was still the lira, the beautiful lira that intoxicated with promises of wealth. Too bad he won't listen to me, my husband. He doesn't want to know anything about the past. He's not interested. It bores him. He wants to drink the future. Luckily I have you now, elephant, and I can vent.

At first, all these memories scared me. I was afraid your big ears would rip the soul from my chest.

But now I feel calm. I can tell that we'll last, you and I.

You and your big ears are the only ones left to listen to my voice. The world has long forgotten me.

It's only you, little elephant, who remembers me, Adua, beautiful Adua. Only you.

5

TALKING-TO

Is that how you greet a relative, Adua? With that look on
your face? Smile. What else have you got teeth for? Smile.
Open that big mouth of yours. And do it quick if you
don't want me to get mad.

6

ZOPPE

Zoppe knew that the best escape route was through his head.

That was the place where he found all the lost scents of his childhood. There, *caano geel, shaah cadees, beer iyo muufo.*

Candied ginger. Marvelous cinnamon. His Wonderland Somalia.

Zoppe thought about all this crouched down on the cold floor of his cell in Regina Coeli. His head between his knees and his thigh anxious against a battered chest. Vertigo and stabbing pain coursed through his tired veins. And his aching limbs felt defeated. He suspected he had two broken ribs. It was hard for him to breathe and even to bend over.

"Those bastards really mangled me."

And as if that weren't enough, they had tossed him unceremoniously in solitary. "This way you'll learn what happens when you mess with us."

Beppe gave him a pat on the head before handing him over to the prison. He touched him like a mother her young. Then he had him sip a yellow liquid.

"Drink, nigger, drink."

Zoppe gulped with difficulty. He made a horrified grimace and felt something burning inside. Was he dying?

Beppe patted him again. "Drink up, you'll feel better."

And Zoppe drank and died once, twice, three times. Then with the fourth sip, the warmth began to reach his spent cheeks.

"My aunt's walnut liqueur can revive even the dead. You'll feel better soon, you'll see," the soldier said, smiling.

In that miserable cell where they'd stuck him there was a cot and a bowl of slop. Limp potatoes floated alongside prickly worms. Zoppe was young, he was famished, but he couldn't bring himself to eat.

"I don't want to shit myself to death in this stinking cell." The room was square, gray, repugnant. Words inscribed with bloody fingernails covered the walls with pain. Zoppe started reading to try to figure out what lay ahead in his increasingly uncertain future.

Mauro da Pisa, Alessandro da Bologna, Antonio da Sassari, Lucio da Roma, Giulio da Pistoia, Simone da Rimini, have all passed through here. The oldest date was 1923. The best inscription was dated 1932. Zoppe recognized it immediately, the supreme poet was one of his favorites:

> Through me is the way to the city of woe.
> Through me is the way to sorrow eternal.
> Through me is the way to the lost below.

"They've never cleaned up, that's clear," he said, addressing an imaginary audience. Actually, he didn't mind the quiet of that isolation. It was a reprieve from the torture, from the senseless beatings that had defiled him down to his soul.

His tormenters would soon appear with their stinking farts and vulgar taunts. But in the meantime there was that strange, rat-scented calm to cradle him.

The pain didn't subside. It was his groin that hurt to death, especially his testicles. Beppe had really beaten him badly. Zoppe asked himself if after all those hits his seed would still be fertile. His testicles throbbed and a yellowish liquid dripped from the tip of his penis. He felt heavy. And he could barely open his puffy eyes.

At the age of twenty he was an old man.

A premature *oday*, with a drooling mouth and achy bones.

He had his visions to comfort him. His mind catapulted him back into the home of Davide the Jew and his little girl, Emanuela.

He had recently been their guests, and the details were still so effervescent and fresh in his mind that he could almost remember without trying.

He could see the sour cherry preserves that Rebecca, Davide's wife, had prepared for dessert. He'd filled up on that delicious tart and had also relished what had come before.

"What is this dish called?" he'd asked, astonished at his overflowing plate.

"It's *rigatoni con la pajata*," Rebecca replied.

Just then Zoppe noted how much mother and daughter resembled each other. The same wide forehead, the same big ears, and those sparkling emerald eyes. But whereas Emanuela was exuberant like all children, Rebecca had something mysterious and seductive about her.

Zoppe envied Davide.

And he said: "It smells good. I envy you this rich dish." Davide accepted that sweet envy.

Looking around, there was really little to be envious of. It was all so small. Even the furniture was tiny. The house was composed of two rooms united by the reddish light that filtered in through a small window. The kitchen with an iron stove was in plain view. In the middle, a table, some tattered chairs and a flesh-toned armchair. The space was packed with furnishings. In every detail there was a certain affinity for symmetry that made such a chaotic space endearing. Zoppe was drawn to a blond walnut cabinet with drawers covered in faux vellum. It was an exquisite object that did not fit well with the overall simplicity. It was a little bit like Rebecca, that cabinet, too refined to be the centerpiece of that set.

Rebecca … Davide … Emanuela …

It was incredible for him to see white Jews. Zoppe had known only Falasha Jews, the Beta Israel, from Lake Tana, even though his father had told him that in the West there were Jews "with skin as pale as the moon." These were pink Jews, so cordial, and their Roman house so cozy and inviting.

Zoppe was blinded by the ochre walls that matched harmoniously with the violet flooring. He was impressed by the hoard of books; they formed a cathedral. And the knickknacks scattered all over the place: ceramic dolls with real hair, decorative wall plates, tasseled colorful boxes and lots of photographs of old people in shiny, faux, silver frames.

Zoppe liked this middle ground where sour cherries intermingled with knowledge.

If he had his basin with him he'd have read the fate of those three people. He would have seen their beginning and their end. All their happiness and their atrocious suffering. Their passionate kisses and betrayals. If only he had his basin he would have warned them about all the dangers and joys of the world.

•

"Water," he requested to the guard. "I'm thirsty."

"Not so fast, Negro," was his answer. "You're not at the Grand Hotel. Learn some manners. You say 'Water, please.'"

"What difference does it make? You people don't have good manners anyway," Zoppe retorted.

"Ah, we've got a rebel here," the guard said. "If times were different," he added, "we would have shown you, you piece of shit. In Regina Coeli we don't like rebels. You're ticks, useless lice of humanity. In Regina Coeli it's easy to die of hunger or thirst, learn that. It's easy to bring down that cocky crest you've got. In Regina Coeli it's a short path to the graveyard. But you're a damned lucky louse. They told me not to let you die. So I'll bring you your water. But mind you, I might not be able to kill you, but put you through hell, that I can do."

Zoppe said nothing. He wanted to smash that fatso's face. But he was in chains. And weak all through his insides. Eventually he ate the slop of potatoes and prickly worms. From the very first bite he could tell that his stomach would refuse to digest it. Vomiting was the logical consequence of an unwanted meal.

Zoppe was a cesspool. The worms dropped from his mouth whole. Restless worms, still alive and a little stunned. He could see them creeping slowly over his wasted body.

"Where's my water?"

He needed to try to sleep. But could one sleep in such a state?

He wondered whether his father, Haji Safar, knew that he was in prison now.

"I'm sure he had a vision." And Zoppe prayed that it hadn't made his father suffer too much.

Happy images from his former life stopped the pain. The lively eyes of his sister, Ayan, his father's gentle hand, the discipline of the Jesuits who had taught him Italian, and the intense letters from his Ethiopian friend Dagmawi Mengiste. They surrounded him and urged him not to give up. He saw their prayers spiral around him in an embrace of courage. "They love me," Zoppe thought, "and they're thinking about me right now." Even the Limentani family was thinking of him.

He could hear the little girl asking her mother, Rebecca, "How do you draw a wildebeest, Mama? Do you think it has the same hump as a camel? Why don't we invite the brown man over for lunch again and ask him to draw one for us?"

Zoppe saw Rebecca's face tensed in a mask of fear. Maybe she knew about him.

Maybe news of his arrest had spread.

He'd ended up in trouble over Francesco Bondi, that Romagnolo with the flat nose and yellow teeth.

Zoppe appreciated nothing about that man. He was too tall, too invasive, too chatty.

He detested the droopy mustache and red hair that the Romagnolo showed off like a trophy. Bondi was always there asking question after question, waiting for amazing answers that Zoppe was never able to give.

And also, he only ever talked about women—bottoms, bosoms, lips, sex. Zoppe found him vulgar. Obviously.

"Do you have a girl?" the Romagnolo often asked. But Zoppe didn't open up.

Of course he had a girl, but he had no intention of telling that guy about it. Asha the Rash was his woman. Every night in his dreams he savored the moment when he would make her his. But he didn't want to share such private thoughts with anyone, let alone that lout Francesco Bondi. He didn't want to sully her beautiful name with a filthy person like him. The Romagnolo ruined women, for sure. Every day he went bragging about his conquests. Mirella, Graziella, Elvira, Carlotta. All of them with big busts and big bottoms. All snatched up under the nose of distracted husbands. These provincial Don Juan routines bored him. He didn't have all that time to waste. He had to work, not dawdle around. Zoppe's greatest desire was to impress his superiors. He wanted honors. He wanted cash. So he had to look active. Lots of work didn't scare him. Especially when he thought of the nice gifts that he would be able to give his Asha the Rash one day.

But then that strange morning came.

Francesco Bondi pounced on him with breath that still smelled of sleep.

Zoppe wasn't alone. In that miserable and miniscule room he was ashamed to call an office, there was a man with yellow hair.

"Hey, Negro," Bondi yelled euphorically. "I saw another Negro like you on the street yesterday. I thought you were the only one in Rome."

Then the Romagnolo noticed the man with the yellow hair. "You're not military," Bondi said, a little irritated. "What are you doing here?"

"Don't judge by appearances. I'm even more, in a sense. The name's Calamaro." The two men shook hands hesitantly.

"And this Negro you saw on the street, what was he like, if I may ask?"

"He was a Negro, what do you think he was like …"

"They're not all the same, did you know that?" said the man with the yellow hair. "There are different types, in every region. Their hair and noses diverge wildly. It depends on the climate."

"Hair? That stuff this guy has on his head, you expect me to call that hair?"

"Yes," said Calamaro, calmly.

"Are you kidding me?"

Zoppe buried his nose in his papers and mentally wandered through the city of Rome in search of the other African Bondi was talking about.

There was definitely Menghistu Isahac Tewolde Medhin. The Eritrean hothead. He ran into him one day around the Pensione Tedeschi on Via Flavia. The Eritrean walked slowly, he didn't worry about being seen too much like Zoppe did. Medhin didn't want to hide, let alone disappear. His movements were filled with pride. He walked with his head high. He had just finished at the Monte Mario international college run by the Methodist Episcopal Church and was trying to figure out what the future held for him. Zoppe didn't like the man. His words were too learned, complicated. And his avid anti-Italian ferocity terrified him. That man would soon get himself into trouble. "I shouldn't have anything to do with him, otherwise he'll ruin me."

As he was lost in these thoughts he saw Francesco Bondi's hand sink into his curly hair.

"You call this hair? This is wool, not even good quality wool!"

"It's hair," Calamaro replied calmly. "It's not pretty, but it's hair. The gentleman is a Negro, but his features are less Negroid than the anthropological specimens I examined in the Congo."

And then he too, no different than Bondi, sank his hand into the hair on Zoppe's exhausted head.

The Somali exhaled with all the strength he had in his lungs and sat there despairingly listening to the two Italians.

He couldn't say exactly when the discussion turned into something more serious. Had it been Bondi who offended Calamaro, or maybe the reverse? Zoppe was confused. He saw only, through his hair, that the two had moved on to hands—their hands. Fists, in short.

"Please, gentlemen," said Zoppe, disconsolate. "Please," he repeated. Then he got the inauspicious idea of trying to break it up.

The police arrested only him for that strange morning brawl.

7

ADUA

A big storm was beating down on our camp when the man with the red beard entered our *tukul*.

That's how things began with my father. That's how I met him, little elephant. That was the last happy day of my life. I was seven or eight years old at most.

I remember that our straw roof was soaked with water and it dripped from every corner of our temporary dwelling.

It was the '60s, but I didn't know that yet. I was just a flea and I struggled with the shaky, provisional nature of our daily life. I was a nomad, a little nomad with a pointy nose and I thought that life was contained in the gleeful bleat of a baby goat. The rain that day was violent. If we held out just a few minutes then it would be paradise.

In the bush, the golden rule during torrential rain is curbing damage at all costs. We all knew that after that brief initial difficulty the sun would come out, even in our hearts. Hope, which had woven the threads of our survival, would never abandon us. A greenish mold, meanwhile, was expanding under our feet. It would bring the worst microbes, the most insidious dangers. But we were used to it. The important thing, as the camp's old madwoman, Howa the Crooked, always said, was to dry the bottoms of your feet well once it had all stopped. *Si fiican u tirtir* was the motto. And already the cloth scraps on our wood *ganbar* were ready. Howa would have appreciated, and maybe even smiled happily about our feverish readiness. Because we truly were happy about the cruel rain that was pounding over our heads. *Wallahi!* So happy. That rain was a true manna from the heavens. Not by chance did everyone's mind go to our rust-colored basins filling up with good rainwater that would quench our thirst in the coming days. Dreams soon gave way to worries of drought.

I was used to rain.

But that man with the red beard jarred with everything. He was so different from the shepherds in our camp. He was as clean and smooth as a young girl.

And his turban had an almost blinding otherworldly glow. Between white and light blue, it was almost frightening.

Then came a sudden thunderbolt.

But instead of coming from the sky, it came from the mouth of the man who until that moment had been the center of my existence.

"Girls, this man is your father," Papa said.

My sister, Malika, and I stood there staring at the man with the red beard. I noticed that he was bowlegged and had a devilish goatee.

And his back was curved like a pregnant woman's. And also, why did Papa introduce him to us as our father?

I wanted to get rid of all of that angst.

"You have to shake his hand. He's your father. Aren't you happy?"

Malika and I were dying to ask, "Aren't you our father?" But neither of us had the nerve. Maybe it was Papa's look, the look of the man who up until that moment we'd considered our father, that dissuaded us. Maybe it was also the eagerness with which he pushed us toward that unfamiliar, lopsided man who inspired no confidence whatsoever. So we kept our mouths shut. As if a crocodile had caught our tongues.

We couldn't even breathe. Or think.

Around us, the bush howled fiercely like it did every night.

I could hear the hyenas cackling and the fierce hunger of their obscene feasts. The crows cawed. The *gorgor* snored.

The lions made love to lionesses worn out with exhaustion. A woman gave birth in pain.

Malika and I stood there, barefoot, between two fathers.

I didn't like the new one at all. He was too old. Too hunched. He had twisted feet, rotten teeth, and the receding chin of a false virgin.

I looked at Papa with a silent plea for help. He broke eye contact and at that moment I realized he was rejecting me.

"Tomorrow you will leave with him for the big city, for Magalo," he said. Leave? For Magalo? Us?

I had heard talk of the big city. Someone had told me that Malika and I were even born there.

I didn't want to go. I sensed that the big city would

swallow all my purity, all my dreams.

I was fine there with my goats, with my camels, and with that golden land that had become part of my bones. The land and I lived for each other. In harmony with the song of the elephants.

I was a nomad. I didn't want to be rooted.

I was a nomad. I wanted to be free to run in the wind.

Malika was different from me. She didn't have many wants, no. All she wanted was for people to love her. She was a person who only had to be given an order and she would follow it. Even the most atrocious order was for her the best possible solution. She refused to think, to decide. She didn't want to be vulnerable. Let other people do that. Her attitude was, My life isn't mine anyway.

So she bowed to this new father. She shook his hand. She signed the pact. She became his slave.

And so with that submissive gesture, she gained his eternal love. I was foaming with rage.

"I don't want to," I shouted. "I want Mama. I want to stay with my people."

Papa told me: "Asha the Rash was your real mother and we aren't your people. Your father, Zoppe, has asked for you. The woman who nursed you is one of my wives. Call her 'god-aunt.' You have different blood in your veins. You must learn this, you must learn it fast. We have been your caretakers."

I didn't want to learn it. I wanted to see the woman who to me would always be my mother. Mama was pretty. She smelled like jasmine.

"I want my mama."

And that was when the bowlegged man broke into that absurd conversation. "Your mother died when she brought you into the world."

"Yes," my ex-father said. "She's dead."

But I'd seen her just a few hours ago.

"But I saw her …" I murmured.

"That's not your mother," the new father yelled.

"But …"

"No 'buts,' you brat. Learn to trust my words. I am the one who brought you into the world."

I looked at my sister with contempt. She had already surrendered to the new order. I couldn't bear such horror.

I saw the old man, the one I would never call father, pick up a thorny branch.

Then he pulled me toward him and gave me two lashes. Two hard lashes. This was my baptism.

The thorns stuck in my skin.

I was like the Christian Jesus, a martyr for sins I hadn't committed. I felt a deep sorrow well up from my unhappy gut.

"Mama, where are you?" I lamented. No one answered.

My papa, the one who had been my papa, left the *tukul*.

I heard his steps rapidly move into the distance. I thought I heard the echo of a sob. "Mama," I called out. Then I fainted.

When I came to, I had become an actress. No one would ever see my real face again.

8

TALKING-TO

Adua, why did you tell your teacher that your name is Habiba? How many times have I told you, your name is Adua? Habiba is the name you had as a nomad, the one that silly romantic of a mother gave you when she was pregnant with you. Habiba is a dirty, filthy name. It's a common name, for a prostitute. Surely my daughter wouldn't have such a common name, would she? Habiba means love in Arabic … bah, I spit on love! There is no such thing as love. It's a useless name, get it into your head. Adua's much better. You should thank me, I named you after the first African victory against imperialism. I, your father, was on the right side. And you must never believe the opposite. I did only the right things in life, only the right things. Not like that good-for-nothing Asha the Rash. The only truly rash thing your mother did was die. She did nothing else, just die. Whereas I, on the other hand, fought alongside the just. Inside your name there's a battle, my battle …

You don't believe me, do you? Do you dare doubt me?

9

ZOPPE

That night Zoppe dreamed about Benito Mussolini's war.

In that muggy dream the war began in a place like so many in the Horn of Africa, where animals were taken out to pasture. A border zone where it was easy to lose your head and fight with the nearby Ethiopians.

The casus belli that Benito Mussolini was yearning for to officially wage war against Ethiopia.

Was it a dream or a vision of the future?

Zoppe had never known how to distinguish between reality and fantasy. He had never learned to manage what he saw very well. Haji Safar had taught him, but he lacked the soul. The second soul that Haji Safar had, the one that allows you to enter into empathy with time.

The second soul.

He was sick of hearing his father say that he didn't have that damned second soul. "I'll make do without! Plus, if you've got money, what do you need an extra soul for?"

Zoppe remembered the smell of sulfur in the dream. Nothing else. He woke up with fright. With the feeling that he'd dreamed something terrible that would perhaps take over his little life too. Something that could be sensed even without a second soul.

"What's all that racket?" the fat guard asked his colleague.

"It's black face going crazy." And then in a strange show of mercy, he said, "Maybe we should give the guy a bath. Otherwise the fleas'll eat him alive."

"Let's take care of it tomorrow," the big one said.

Zoppe scratched his head. What time was it? How long had he slept? Was it daytime or the middle of the night?

He suspected that making him lose his sense of orientation was part of a plan. They wanted him to drive him crazy.

Zoppe curled back up in the cot. He closed his eyes and began to summon a vision. The first image that came to him was his sister, Ayan, looking for red peppers in the Warta Nabbada souk in Magalo. "That means someone at home is making stew today and the good fragrant *injera* with the holes that the Ethiopians showed us how to make." Zoppe preferred Ethiopian to Somali injera. Yes, he really disliked the Somali kind. It was small, meager, dry. The Ethiopian kind was sour and soft. With the Ethiopian kind, sauce, any sauce, absorbed deep down. Whereas with the Somali kind, sauce slid off without the least resistance. It was hard for him to admit that Ethiopians were better at making injera, but it was the truth.

But with rice and meat, Zoppe consoled himself, there's no contest. The *bariis iskukaris* we make is the best

on earth. Bariis iskukaris, where the meat, rice, and cardamom blend together to satisfy palates ready to drown in a
sea of perdition. Ah, bariis iskukaris … Zoppe wondered
if he would ever eat it again.

Nothing but slop, worms, in that cell.

Meanwhile his sister, Ayan, was looking for potatoes at
the market stalls.

The cell filled with different aromas and concentric
visions. Zoppe didn't dare reopen his eyes for fear that
they would leave him too soon. He had to keep them
there with him in that dark cell as long as possible. He
needed their company, their comfort.

And then the *cadar* which Somali women use to perfume themselves began to mix in with the myrrh that
Asha the Rash used to make their environment more
pleasant. And then the cinnamon, incense, sandalwood,
golden amber, passionflower, ripe mango, healthy papaya,
sensuous pineapple.

Somalia was a step away.

He just had to grab it. He just had to dream it.

And from Somalia he was catapulted to a back street in
the Prati quarter of Rome.

·

All it took was a glance at her face to see how much she
was suffering. Poor, sweet little Rebecca.

She was a vision too. A stronger, more incarnate vision.
Almost real.

"Why have you come to see me, woman? Why here in this cell?" Zoppe wanted to ask the vision, but ultimately he said nothing, because he already knew the answer.

"You're a wizard, right?" Rebecca's shadow asked. Zoppe never liked to answer questions with a yes or no.

Certainties were the devil's daughters. He was well aware. Salvation lay only in doubt. In that middle ground where the gears rebelled against the master clockmaker. But she needed him. She was so desperate.

"I'm a seer, or rather, my father is, and my dear aunt too. I see things, but I don't have the gift. I see but I don't know what to do with my visions. I feel the vibrations of the universe. I read the world, but I don't know how to decipher it."

Suddenly, Rebecca's eyes lit up with interest. "What do you mean?"

"Just what I said," replied Zoppe.

"And what am I now? Why am I here?"

"I don't know," Zoppe replied slowly. "That depends on you."

"I'm in bed and I'm dreaming. And in the dream I find myself in this foul cell. And in the left corner there are five dead rats. I'm afraid of rats, even dead ones. But now I have no urge to scream. I don't feel afraid here."

Zoppe couldn't say anything to that shadow. Say that he was the one who wanted to see her. That maybe it was only his dream, a projection. He couldn't say that he found her beautiful, fascinating, enchanting, that he desired her as much as, sometimes more than, Asha the Rash. That he'd dreamed of her naked, white, pure, almost every night since first seeing her at her little house in Prati. And that he envied her husband, the giant Davide, for all the orgasms given and received, for all the sighs, for the intimate conversations whispered at dawn.

There was also another reason he couldn't tell her anything. The woman was in danger, Zoppe could feel it. Aside from desire, he felt a boundless sorrow for her.

But things were changing, everything was changing. Zoppe could feel it in the air.

There was a hostility toward the Jews that with every day became more overt, more bold-faced, more hateful.

•

It was Aunt Bibi who, years before, had taught him to read animal entrails.

He never called her "aunt," just Bibi. In Swahili, "bibi" means Mrs., lady. She was the lady of the house, of hearts and of reclamation. It was Bibi who presided, giving orders at the *xus* for our ancestors and hosting the commemorative *zab*. She was the one who decided which goats to buy, in what order to butcher them.

Zoppe saw himself as a little boy again in Bibi's yard. He was maybe four or five, playing with a baby goat full with milk. The kid had suckled hungrily from the maternal teat only a moment before, and now, like any other little one, she just wanted to enjoy the company of the butterflies fluttering lazily around her tail. She was pretty, the little goat, sweet. Little Zoppe wanted to cover her with kisses. Pet her soft coat. And learn her uncertain language made of high and low *baaaas*. What he would have given to understand her, to talk to her. She would have been so charming. She had a lively face, all round and soft.

But without warning, Bibi broke through that explosion of affection. His aunt, with her great stature and necessary cruelty put an end to the idyll between the little boy and the baby goat.

"Get out of the way, you little *balaayo*," and with a push, she shoved him away. "But we were playing …" stammered Zoppe.

"She's done playing," and she grabbed her by the neck with her plump, capable hands.

Zoppe remembered her stunned eyes, her confusion, her increasingly tortured bleats. "Where is this big woman taking me?" those sweet eyes asked. And Zoppe didn't have the heart to answer that sweet little goat. How could he admit to her that beyond that yard there was nothing but death awaiting her?

He suddenly felt cold. And he started convulsively rubbing his body.

"Help her, Lord, when the blade enters her." He sat down and curled up, in wait. And he waited to hear the last cry of his dear friend.

The cry of death did not take long to arrive.

Hours later, the goat's insides were presented at lunch. Zoppe was surrounded by ravenous mouths waiting to feast.

Zoppe was a good boy. And tears fat as bushels of hay ran down his smooth, oval face.

"What is it, sweet boy?" Bibi said.

"It's …" and he couldn't manage to finish the sentence.

"You don't like it? This is a special dish, you know. The goat is nourished on its mother's milk until the very end. Then, once the animal is butchered, the intestine is removed while it's still full of milk and mother's love. The intestine has to be removed very carefully, otherwise it will break. Then you cook it and make *baug*, which is like the cheese *gaal* make. Infidel's cheese. A stringy paste that melts in your mouth."

Little Zoppe hesitated before the steaming tray. Could he really eat a friend?

Then his aunt stuck a piece in his mouth. And he melted at the taste of those succulent entrails.

He felt like a murderer.

"She died for a good cause, don't be sad for her. Everyone dies sooner or later."

Sooner or later …

And that was when Bibi told him: "Look at the folds on the insides. From them, you can read the world."

A deep scar lined those soft mounds.

"I don't see anything. It's all mixed up."

"Look, son, look harder. Don't you see that stretch of the road to Galkayo? Don't you see a man carrying a bundle? And don't you see the horrible vulture lurking overhead? Don't you see the sky laden with promise? Don't you see the hyena giving birth in pain? Don't you see the children on the pasture? Don't you see the sweet bulbul bird that cheers the heavens? Observe that scar, smell the fresh baug. Get nice and close. Let yourself go. There is the *aliif* and the *taa*. The *miim* and the *ra*. The *saad* and the *daad*, the *shiin* and the *siin*." Bibi enumerated the letters of the alphabet, showed them to me in the entrails. "Here you'll find the writing of the world and little by little you too will learn to decipher it."

Zoppe moved his nose close to the plate. And he smelled a strange odor of aged cheese.

He looked at the scar again. And he saw her, the little goat. She was skipping around happily and the butterflies gaily joined in.

"You're grown up now, my boy. We are the descendants of tribes that have been lost in the night of time. And the history that runs through us has brought more knowledge to our already full treasury. And today, you have become a *faaliyaha*, a soothsayer. Sweet boy, none of us can escape his destiny. Now eat your baug, otherwise it'll get cold."

"What a fine destiny," thought little Zoppe, and he dug in.

10

ADUA

"Tell the stories you have, as best you can."

That's not my quote, it's from a famous writer. I didn't know who he was. But yesterday I flipped through one of his books at the grocery store. I opened it randomly and that line popped out. I read it a few times. At first I didn't even understand it much. But then something in my gut told me that maybe that random sentence had more to do with me than I could imagine. I frantically dug through my purse for money. In hard times one has to do things a certain way. Every cent has its weight. The fact is, I wanted that book so badly. I really, really wanted it. I grabbed the story collection with both hands. To give me some motivation, infuse my tired veins with a little courage. I was trembling. In the end the book cost me nineteen euros. That meant giving up my wheat semolina, chunks of squash, citron soda, and new potatoes.

I didn't buy anything I needed to buy. No liquids, no solids. I bought pages.

The shelves filled with delights looked out at me disconsolately, a little shocked. I was abandoning them. The pistachios were dejected, the spreads sad, the mustard prey to an entirely new panic. Was I really abandoning them?

Meanwhile, the book did a polka in my green bag. Happy to have a new owner, a new house, a new reader.

Meanwhile, I thought of my little husband all full of spunk. The young man "Made in Lampedusa" who I got on sale anyway.

What would I make for him that night? "I'll give him yesterday's leek soup."

My boy has a healthy appetite. He likes everything I make him.

It's hunger, the hunger he suffered crossing the Sahara desert, that makes him as docile as a little lamb.

He's not one of those brutes who expect steak every day. He's just as happy with the stew of leftover vegetables I make in lean times. By the end of the month meat is too much of a luxury for us. But no one will take our roasted half-goat with potatoes at the beginning of the month away from us. Then he sucks every bone dry like a teat full of milk.

The only thing my little one can't give up is *shaah*, our cardamom, cinnamon and clove tea. When he drinks it he sweats like a pig, but then I see him shine with an entirely different light inside. When he's in a good mood he even pours in a little milk and makes a shaah cadees that takes him back to childhood.

I don't drink cadees anymore. It ruins your figure. Gives you cellulite.

Gets you with water retention.

But when my little husband, my sweet little Titanic, sips a brimming cup of it sprawled out in front of the TV, I confess, I feel jealous.

So much nostalgia for old times.

My father, Mohamed Ali Zoppe, liked cadees too. I'm sure it was the excessive amounts of sugar he put in it that led him to death. Diabetes had turned him into a swollen, noxious blob. So I was told—I wasn't there when he passed, between flatulence and regret. But my father always added a dash of ginger to his cadees. He said that *sanjibiil* "reinvigorates the manhood and warms the muscles." I don't know if ginger works like Viagra. But as far as warming goes, it works. On cold winter nights it's a lifesaver. I recommend it, my little elephant. Yes, a real lifesaver.

The first time I saw my father, or Zoppe as I called him at the time, adding ginger was at the house of Hajiedda Fardosa, one of his wives. My mother, Asha the Rash, as I found out later, was the first. But when she died bringing me into the world she was immediately replaced by a girl with braids and her first period. So I was told. That night, that first night when I saw him add ginger, I'll never forget.

He had dragged us from the bush to the city by the sea, tearing us away from what I thought of as my family, my mama.

I'm speaking for myself, because of course Malika, my sellout of a sister, had followed along meekly.

That night, that cursed night, was the first of my new life. Hajiedda Fardosa lived in the city by the sea.

Magalo was a port city, one of the many on the southeastern coast of Somalia. "Here are your roots," he told us. "It is here that you will bring your glory." Magalo wasn't as big as Mogadishu, but it wasn't a two-bit town either. Magalo had schools, offices, a nice big city hall, several mosques, a Catholic church, a library, a branch of the central university, a bookstore, a pasta factory, two markets, a stationery store, four cafes, three restaurants, a hardware store, two boutiques, three tailors, a dry cleaner, and lots of other things. It was in Magalo that real life happened. In order to be somebody you had to be a part of that cursed homeland. And Magalo had a sea that took your breath away.

Only there did the Indian Ocean roar with pleasure. Only there did the whales come to make love at sunset.

At first I didn't like Magalo. For me, it was a usurper. One who wanted to take the place of my adored little goats. One who had torn me away from my parents, the people I loved most in the world.

It was hate at first sight between me and Magalo.

Magalo was the end of a life, an ominous change of destiny.

And Magalo was also home to Hajiedda Fardosa. I don't remember much about that fateful first night. Except one detail. On the ground I saw a female lion skin. It seemed alive and so proud of being the most beautiful. The coat was intact. A perfect shade of gold. I felt sorry for her. I had seen many in the bush. They were vicious and blood-thirsty. But there was something magical in their wandering. Nothing like the dirty, vulgar hyenas we always had to deal with. The lionesses' stride was that of precarious nobility fighting against scarcity and bullets. The stride of a queen whose crown had been stolen by a male.

I looked like that skinned lioness. I too was proud and trapped. Proud and confined in the baroque house of the revered fat wife.

I remember that night, that unforgettable night; the pungent odor of burned myrrh pervaded the air. It made me sneeze and I felt the strange specter of fear hover like a vulture over my live carcass.

"You'll have to civilize them," my father told Hajiedda Fardosa. "They're savages. Especially the taller one."

And that was when, after those cutting words, I saw him add a pinch of ginger to his shaah cadees.

11

TALKING-TO

Adua, go apologize to your sister right now. Who taught you to be so wild? Is it your desk mate teaching you these things? Starting tomorrow you won't speak another word to her. Who knows what she put in your head. You're like your mother, Asha, you trust everyone around you. The world is cruel, Adua, you shouldn't trust anyone. Now be off. I believe I've made myself clear.

12

ZOPPE

Everyone was waiting for Maria Uva.

Eyes glued to the cliff. Spirits in nervous anticipation. "Will she be wearing our tricolor?" Orazio Civa asked Zoppe.

"Maybe," the Somali said with little enthusiasm.

"Ah, Maria Uva, they say you're as beautiful as a siren."

"Sirens, mister," Zoppe said disdainfully, "are dangerous creatures, especially here in Port Said."

"But I'm as strong as Odysseus, Zoppe my friend, there's no siren who could resist me; Maria should watch out. And I want to immortalize her in my notebook. Up to now I've only drawn birds and a few wayward fish. A pretty lady would be a nice addition, don't you think?"

Civa had a nice smile and eyes that recalled the forests of Europe's far north. A handsome fellow, dark hair, refined bearing, medium height, and biceps that not even the Laocoön at the Vatican Museums could match.

Civa's looks were something that emerged gradually, with time and a certain dose of perseverance. He wasn't a heartthrob out of a romantic melodrama, listless and vain. He didn't have the sparkle of someone like Rudolph

Valentino. He was more like Amedeo Nazzari, a man to be discovered frame by frame. But women are impatient. And a good-looking man like that found himself all alone sighing over a mirage that was about to appear over an Egyptian cliffside.

Maria Uva.

Frenzy over Maria Uva, the patriot Maria, the mature, plump Italian woman the legionnaires pined for. The one with the high-pitched voice who saluted the future soldiers in the war that fascism was preparing for.

"She'll come out soon, I want to be ready, my heart is already racing for her." Zoppe studied the young man and found him a mix of contradictions.

His sentimentality didn't fit well with his blind and total loyalty to the National Fascist Party that he loved showing off at society events.

Civa said that Benito Mussolini was a beacon, the light of all knowledge. He also claimed that he would swallow even the bitterest pill for his *Duce*.

But then there was that dissonant note in his crystalline voice. The one that made you doubt his loyalty to fascism.

You would stare at his light eyes to figure out the truth, but they knew exactly how to evade scrutiny.

But Zoppe didn't care whether the boy was a fascist or not. To him, he was a tool, the weapon that destiny had provided him to free him from his jailers. In the end he was grateful to Civa. Without his help he would have probably been left to rot in that hovel, Regina Coeli.

It had all happened so fast that day, the day he was freed, months ago.

One of his guards, the bigger one, had come over and said to him, "Negro, we have to wash you today." And his colleague added as a little joke, "Maybe rubbing you with soap will turn you white."

That morning, besides the promise of being clean there was also a timid ray of sunlight penetrating the cell to cheer him.

Rome was covered in pink dust.

Maybe the tramontane is coming, the old people said.

.

"Cat got your tongue?" asked a sergeant whom Zoppe had never seen before.

The room was full of light and Zoppe had been dumped there unceremoniously by the guards.

Finally clean, shaven, groomed, he felt like he could meet the soldier's gaze. That irked the sergeant.

"There's someone outside who has come to collect you. You will finish your sentence in the service of the distinguished Count Anselmi, a father of the nation, a more illustrious fascist would be hard to find. The count wants you. He insisted on having you, you know. In no time at all he moved heaven and earth, you know how these counts are, and in a certain sense he bought you. Your fate was decided at the highest levels. Thank your saints. Be glad. You were lucky, louse, keep that in mind.

You earned yourself an entirely different destiny and you know it. But the count wants you and there's nothing I can do about it."

The sergeant gritted his teeth at that last sentence.

Zoppe remembered Haji Safar's words. *"Qofkii aammuso waa dhintay."* He who chooses silence is already dead.

And he decided that even if the battle was lost, he could at least try to fight the future ahead of him.

He didn't want to die a count's slave.

"But …" He had trouble getting the words out. "But, sir, I can't go into the service of a count. I have a job to finish at the base, in Rome."

A thunderous laugh filled the room, burying his minute words.

In that same room were also the three goons who had beaten him days ago. "Are they going to start up again?" he wondered.

He felt a pang in his chest and a pitiful creak between his balls. That's where Beppe had hit him the hardest.

"Here are your friends. Aren't you happy to see them again?" To distract himself from that miserable sight his eyes began to wander. A lone portrait of Benito Mussolini stood out on the wall. No trace of the king.

"Maybe," Zoppe wondered, "they forgot about the king?"

It was a sad room. The gray walls gave it a touch of claustrophobia, which rendered every sensation stagnant. No flowers, no family photos, not even scratch paper with doodles or stubby pencils for company. A layer of pink dust remained the single sign of life.

"For a while, boy, you're done with the base."

"But ... if ... that is, that's the only reason I'm here, to translate, they sent me specially. Has anyone notified the priests?"

"Forget about your Jesuits. Erase them from your memory. Only they could dump a Negro like you in Rome. And to translate what? There's no war yet. You would have been useful later. Right now you're only in the way. We tolerate Father Evaristo's little priests because the Vatican gave us strict orders to do so, and it's trouble if you ruffle a single hair on their heads. But we've got their number, oh yes, we do."

Zoppe sank to the floor like a rag.

"Come on, don't be like that. We don't want to hurt you. Consider this a little chat among friends."

Zoppe's hand instinctively went to shield his groin. He would defend his manhood even if it cost his life. They wouldn't leave him sterile. Death would be better. And he had promised Asha the Rash, beautiful Asha, that he would come back to Magalo and marry her.

Zoppe bit his tongue.

And he began mentally reciting a prayer, one he had known since childhood, that had the ancestral power of driving away the evil spirits that whispered horrors in the heart of creation.

"We found an interesting photo among your personal effects." Photo? They'd searched his room.

"Pretty girl, this one. How old is she? Nine? Ten? Her chest isn't too developed yet, I see … hmm …"

Ayan, his sister.

What chest was this guy talking about? She was still a child. He felt a wave of disgust.

The photo was from a year ago. Ayan had an innocent, expectant look. Braids close-knit like ants framed a perfectly oval head. And her big lips were bursting with stories and laughter.

She was pretty and sweet, his sister.

One day, like a good brother, he would give her away to the best of men. But now, Zoppe wondered, would he live long enough to keep that promise? What would Ayan do without her brother?

If those three fascists went back to work on him, he wouldn't live through it. "Your sister, right? We know."

Zoppe shivered. *Please, not Ayan, Lord, save her from his madness.*

Not a single muscle on his face betrayed his concern. Zoppe opened his big dark eyes wide to show them he wasn't afraid and that their threats had no effect on him.

But his temples throbbed and his stomach juices jetted into his esophagus. Back straight, chin out, eyes fixed, shoulders wide.

"It would be a shame if something happened to this little girl, don't you agree?" and then he snapped his fingers with a sound that to Zoppe was louder than the bells of St. Peter's.

Snap. Snap. Snap.

Beppe stepped forward.

The scene went by so fast that Zoppe had almost no time to figure out what was happening.

Beppe unzipped his fly, pulled out his penis, rubbed it for a minute and then released his warm spunk all over little Ayan's photo.

"Ugh, what a careless soldier," the sergeant said. "It would be a shame if something like this happened to your sister, wouldn't it?"

Zoppe was shaken, but his face remained impassive.

"She's at Via Cardinal Massaia, in the Littorio Quarter … the one you Somalis have the nerve to call Warta Nabbada."

Via Cardinal Massaia … no one called it that. Everyone knew that was Haji Safar's street, the street of the soothsayers and storytellers. That was where the stars were studied and worlds were glimpsed in the eyes of newborns.

The Italians had stuck some unknown cardinal's name on it. There was a Via Cardinal Massaia in Mogadishu too, in Xamar Weyne, right in the middle of the marketplace.

The name was an abuse in Mogadishu too.

13

ADUA

There was a small movie theater in Magalo, the fascists built it in the '30s—an ideal vehicle, they thought, for colonial propaganda. There were several in Somalia. Ours was a movie theater intended for the local population. It was so run down, with busted seats and a sheet metal roof, nothing compared to the Cinema Xamar in Mogadishu, with its austere Mussolinian structure. Magalo's little cinema had no pretensions—it was plain, subdued, almost hidden. The people loved it, it felt like it belonged to them, like the well in the center of the city, the city hall, the livestock market, the goldsmith square. When the Italians left in 1960, a magnate born in the old quarter of Xafad, a man named Idris Shangani, decided to restore it. Idris Shangani was one of those Somalis who had made money during colonialism by sending bodies to the front during Italy's war against Ethiopia. Then after the end of World War II, when the United Nations decreed that Italy and the newly-formed Trust Territory of Somaliland would ferry us to independence, Mr. Shangani got even richer.

"He was a crook, that one!" my father repeated daily at lunch.

"He was a collaborator, they're the worst." He trembled as he said that word, his voice broken, fragmented. A tremor went through his whole body, turning him to jelly. My father grew agitated and spit on the ground, his mouth filled with curses and insults for the figure who in his eyes incarnated the greatest sin.

But these outbursts were rare for him, because Father didn't like to talk about the past.

Yes, he preferred to keep quiet.

Sure, Mr. Shangani was a crook, but how lucky we'd been to have him as a fellow citizen of Magalo! Without his money we would have never known about the existence of Ava Gardner or Norma Jean. The movies they showed were dated, but in Magalo, where there'd never been anything of the sort, those old films dubbed with literal translations from Italian were manna from the heavens. In Magalo, thanks to the big screen, the women had an hour every day to dream. They lined up after the *Dhuhr* prayer, only after stuffing their fat husbands with food. They never managed to see a whole film, they didn't have time. At home there was the mending, ironing, cleaning, cooking, nursing the children, bathing the grandparents. They went to the little cinema just to catch a few frames, a few fleeting details. In fifteen minutes they'd decided whom they loved and hated. Lots of them needed just five minutes, the minimum to get lost in the blue eyes of a fleeting Paul Newman. The virgins of Magalo, however, preferred Gregory Peck. And they were all crushed when, almost without a fight, he let go of that sweet flower Audrey Hepburn ... And then there were cowboys and Indians, every little boy's favorite. It took only a moment to turn a movie into a shared game played on Magalo's blistering sands. Most cheered for the Indians, of course, which makes sense—they were more impressive. They had trouble relating to John Wayne. "He waddles like a pig," the kids yelled. And on the blistering beaches they made a show of imitating the heavy walk that made Wayne look like a freshly infibulated girl, the stitches still enflaming her tender vagina. No, no, the Indians were better. They had boundless bravery and those fantastic feathers.

Yea for the redskins, down with the John Waynes!

Magalo's little cinema was called *Il Faro*, The Lighthouse, or *Munar* as we say in Somali.

In fact everything was a munar, in Magalo. Everything was a reminder of the great labor of our forefather Torobow, who had erected the tower that later became our city's beacon by his strength alone. In Magalo, wherever you went, you saw a lighthouse. There was the Munar nightclub, the Munar grocery, the Munar Italian bakery, Munar Square.

Our lighthouse was considered, like the one on Cape Guardafui, one of Somalia's historic monuments.

My father no longer liked the lighthouse after it was modified in the thirties. "They defaced us," he would say.

But if you asked him to elaborate he shied away like a virgin at her first kiss. The additional element Papa hated so much was the blade of an axe. With that, Torobow's

Moorish tower was transformed into a grandiose *fasces lictoriae*, the bundle of rods symbolizing fascist power.

"For the perpetual glory of Rome," was inscribed on the base. For me, reading that inscription made me long for that faraway Rome, full of *la dolce vita* and cabaret.

I didn't understand fascism then.

The memory of it was already gone. And you would always find people like Idris Shangani who would happily tell you how life wasn't so bad under the Italians. Usually it was a former *askari* or a *madama* who hadn't minded being a kept woman. But how could a little thing like me understand those details? One master is as good as another, that was the gist. And Magalo wasn't Mogadishu; in Magalo, history went by at an angle. There was no Abdullahi Issa, the spirit of Somali independence, to educate us. To explain to the little people of Magalo that the value of our land lay in us, African citizens, architects of our own destiny. No one had ever told us that colonialism was the problem. Even those who knew the truth said nothing. My father, for example, said nothing.

He muttered a few things, comments so vague they didn't express, they didn't explain. I was a little girl, I didn't think about political matters.

I wanted to be like Norma Jean. I didn't care about the rest. I wanted the lights, the makeup, the awards, the red carpets, the passionate kisses.

I wanted to dream, dance, fly. I wanted to escape. Italy was everywhere in my life.

Italy was kisses, holding hands, passionate embraces. Italy was freedom. And I so hoped that it would become my future. In Magalo, before the socialist nationalist Siad Barre came to power, lots of Italians lived in the city. You would see them strolling down the main boulevard in their elegant clothes at sundown. Perfect ties and cufflinked sleeves. Women often sported pretty little hats that transformed their petite frames into proud and beautiful Grace Kellys. The Italians opened restaurants and gelato shops. The wealthiest had banana plantations just outside the city. At school, among us girls, we would talk about their beautiful houses and the legions of servants they had looking after them. We were jealous, I admit it. And more than one dreamed of marrying an Italian when she grew up.

It was Papa who dragged me and Malika to the Munar cinema for the first time. We had been in Magalo for a month when it happened. The trauma of separation was still fresh. The wound still raw. The bush was still there, frozen in front of my dark eyes.

Papa Zoppe hated Mr. Shangani, but he loved cinema too much to deprive himself of such a joy.

That day, when we came home from school, he told us: "Tonight we're all going to the cinematograph." He was happy. I was not. I was alone, terribly alone.

I missed the goats and in my dreams I cried for my mama, the woman I'd thought was my mother.

"Mama, rescue me," I called out to her. "Mama, help me," I begged. But the nights went by and no one came.

Only the broken coo of romancing owls soothed my fitful sleep.

Especially at night, I couldn't accept my new condition as a city girl, even if with every day my body was slowly adapting to the sweet seductions of a too-comfortable life. I was getting used to it—almost without noticing— to silence, a soft mattress, and morning breakfast, injera with melted butter and sugar. The rhythm of my life was marked by the call of the muezzin and the school bell. I didn't have to worry about hyenas and lions anymore. And in the bright midday sky, sweet birds chirped. The vultures, horrid flying vermin, were just a memory.

"I love it here," my sister Malika once said to me. I spit in her face. The betrayal didn't come as a surprise, but it hurt. It hurt badly. It was a hurt that was overwhelming and full of anger.

The night we went to the cinema, the old man had in mind celebrating Malika's tenth birthday. It had just rained and the frogs covered the earth in a cloak of green. The silly things had emerged from their burrows to take advantage of the sudden cool. Slick and jumpy, they basked in the last drops of the rainy season.

"Remember, stay in your seats. And don't move," our father told us. "Especially when the lights go off. You'll bother the others."

"All right, Father," my sister said. I nodded slightly.

"There's nothing to be afraid of, but if you disobey you'll get a taste of my *karbaash*."

The karbaash—we'd heard about that. It may have been Hajiedda Fardosa herself who put us on guard. A karbaash was a whip used for donkeys.

We entered the theater. And we sat down, Malika and I, as we'd been instructed. Then I suddenly felt a tug on one of my braids. My heart jumped.

"Ow," I said. It was Sultana Patel, my Indian classmate, sitting behind me. There were lots of Indians in Magalo.

"Don't you know I'm with my father? If you make me yell you'll get me in trouble. We have to be quiet, you know!"

"I'm not dumb," she replied. "I saw him get up. And what's the big deal if you talk to me? The movie hasn't started yet."

I froze. I wondered if it was a good idea to explain to my new friend that I didn't know what was going to happen in the room. What was a movie? And how could you tell when it started?

I was embarrassed. I had so many questions I wanted to ask Sultana, so pretty and kind, my only friend. But I didn't want her to laugh at me. Discover my ignorance. "Have you seen the Maciste movies?"

"No, you?"

"Yeah," she replied. "They're boring though. There's a guy, the star, who thinks about nothing but battle, from start to finish. No love scenes, kisses, pretty clothes … Of course, I love Nadira. She dances a lot. I learn a new step from every one of her movies."

"Oh," I remarked as if I had understood. I was hopeless. I had to get out of the conversation, as quickly as possible.

"Promise you'll teach me to dance." My tone was peremptory.

"Promise," she murmured. I looked at her.

She was beautiful.

Her mother had gathered her long silky hair into a bun, which she'd decorated with a garland of flowers. The white petals reflected the colorful bundle of the sari that Sultana wore with elegance and ease. It was the first time I'd seen her in a sari. At school we wore uniforms: pants and white shirts. But now we were at the cinema and Sultana looked beautiful.

I felt so ugly.

I looked at myself and sadly noticed how monotone I was. Scruffy braids, a potato sack as my only good clothes, half-broken clogs that were a humiliating sight. I was as dingy as a defective lamp.

Despite everything Sultana smiled at me, as if she really liked me.

"Okay, we'll start with a few steps." Then her smile faded. "Hey, your dad is coming. We'll talk about it at school, sister."

We were partners in crime, true friends. I was happy, but my nerves didn't go away.

The movie was coming and I had no idea what a movie was.

The lights in the theater went out. My father, with his

long, henna-red beard, turned and said to me, "Remember, don't get up for any reason. And you'll be in trouble if you wet your pants."

Dark. Then in succession the sea, a sunset, music so loud it hurt my ears, words bigger than in the textbooks at school and a sense of anticipation that shook my soul. It was the first time I'd ever seen the sunset without the muezzin calling us to the *Maghrib* prayer. That plastic sunset almost seemed sacrilegious. Born of the son of Satan. I was frightened. I looked at my father and Malika. But they seemed immune to the terror that was consuming me inside, entranced by the words that ran before our eyes.

Then the voice came. It was Italian but at the time I wasn't very familiar with the language. But I was able to understand that long ago someone called Ulysses had tricked a sorceress called Circe—what a pretty name! There were unusual names going around at school too. There was a Mario in our class and a Ginevra. Skin pink like the pulp of a ripe grapefruit. Red like watermelon when the teacher called on them. Ginevra and Mario often changed colors. Sometimes they were green, especially when they caught cold, or white, when they were really startled. They were funny, with their rainbow. And unlucky. Unlike me, who was always brown.

Sultana was brown too, but not as dark. Sometimes she changed color too. Mario and Ginevra more, though.

As I was lost in these thoughts, a woman in a blue dress

appeared on the screen, on some kind of strange boat very different from the ones I had seen in Magalo. The woman seemed to be wearing a kind of sari. But her shoulders were covered by a light veil, much like the *garbasaar* our Somali women wear. But that blue-clad figure had just appeared when the scene changed. No longer the sea, but a gloomy, dark place like one of my nightmares where the vultures devoured my goats. I closed my eyes for a while and it felt like an eternity. When I opened them again there was the woman in blue with two men next to her. One was nearly naked. He had a leopard-print cloth covering his privates and lots of muscles he showed off very proudly. To his left, there was a strange white man with stuff all over his face and body.

I wondered if Maciste, that blond in the loincloth, at the end of this thing everyone called a movie, would come out of the screen to greet us.

To me, that night, all that fiction seemed a reality. But a reality that was better than my present one.

I don't know when it happened, but as the story went on and the characters multiplied, my fear began to fade.

By the time the movie was halfway through I was completely won over. That night I didn't dream of the bush. No goats, no mama, no rains, no vultures. There was just Maciste to soothe me. His hair blond like the horizon.

I slept soundly.

And Magalo no longer seemed like such a horrible place.

14

TALKING-TO

Adua, come here, now. Don't make me lose my patience. What's the meaning of this? Come on, out with it. Why am I sending you to school, eh? To read this junk? What is this? Come on, answer! I'll tell you what it is: crap! It's a photo novel, paper full of foolishness. Love is nonsense. Love, Adua, doesn't exist, better get it in your head now. Don't be like your fool of a mother Asha the Rash, she really believed in love. She called her outbursts love and disgraced us all by dying. The neighbors say I killed her by leaving her alone while she was pregnant. They say she died of love, of love for me.

Have you ever heard such colossal nonsense? Dying for love, as if that were possible. She died, your mother, because she was a fool, to spite me. I won't have you, my daughter, go down the same road to perdition. Get all your photo novels and bring them to me. We'll burn them. We'll make a nice bonfire. That way you'll see what happens with love. Love, my child, always goes up in smoke.

15

ZOPPE

"Maria, come out, I love you!" "Maria, I worship you!" "Maria, you're gorgeous!" "Sing me something, Maria! Please, sing me something. I left my girl back at home and I'm homesick."

"Maria, will there really be war?"

"Maria, bless me in case I die, I'll die happy thinking of you!"

Zoppe couldn't understand the *gaal*. They were all huddled at the steamship landing to see that woman decked out in the Italian flag, greeting the legionnaires about to leave for East Africa.

"The war is coming soon," said a soldier on his right.

"And Maria Uva is going to boost our spirits for all the hardships we'll have to face."

Zoppe's desire to run from that landing was strong. What did he have to do with those pink people and their dirty colonial war?

Avenge Adua, stand on the side of the empire, make way for the virility of Rome … He pissed on that propaganda.

All he wanted from the Italians was the money to buy a big house in Skuraran for his Asha.

Everything else was of no consequence to him.

"What am I doing here?" Zoppe asked himself, watching the throng of Italians grow on the unsteady steamship landing. The Italians clamored, waving their hands, sending their enamored sighs toward the bare cliffside.

Oh, Maria, love me, take me, hold me, kiss me, squeeze me, smother me. Pray for us sinners, Maria, now and in the hour of our death.

Amen.

•

Zoppe was hot and his head was fuming. Getting all worked up over some whore, especially one who was pudgy and plain. That Maria Uva must have had some advantage. Maybe she earned money from these shows for the troops, or was even the kept woman of some big fish in the regime.

Meanwhile, the clamor continued.

The soldiers confused their hard-ons with the old catechism lessons they'd learned by heart as children.

And any Maria Uva would rise up in their hearts as if she were the Virgin Mary in the flesh. A sister, a mother, a wife, a goddess.

Maskiin … Zoppe thought. Poor kids. Was this how Italy betrayed its youth?

Zoppe felt his breath falter on that landing heavy with sighs. The pungent odor of cheap cologne combined with the soldiers' smelly armpits was making him woozy.

Maria, Maria, Maria …

Come out, love, sing for us, blessed are you among women. Was bringing out some hairy old cunt all it took to convince them that Benito Mussolini's war was good and just?

•

When Maria Uva appeared on the rocks, the cries of the worked up men drowned out the sound of the sea. A wave of repressed manhood crashed over the bulkheads and every surface was bathed in desire. Maria Uva's voice was shrill, high, almost irritating. But for those little soldiers the show was paradise.

It was in that moment of general captivation that Rebecca appeared to Zoppe.

The vision was clear. There was Rebecca, and she was holding her little girl's stuffed bear.

"I didn't think you would cross the sea," Zoppe said. "I thought I wouldn't dream of you anymore."

"How are you?"

"I don't know."

The vision started growing dimmer and Rebecca's face less clear.

"Atrocious news is coming," she merely said. "My husband minimizes it, almost doesn't notice. He keeps talking about his father who died fighting in Vittorio Veneto, his uncle Nathan's medal of honor. He's a nationalist, my Davide. Just the other day he told me, 'If Mussolini goes to war with the Abyssinians, it would be nice to enlist and go to East Africa.'"

"There's money in this war."

"But don't you feel pity for your people? Don't you feel pity for the deaths it will cause?"

"Money is the only thing that really counts in this life. You can't wipe your behind with pity and I need to get married. There's a woman waiting for me down in my country."

"A woman? Really?"

"If I gather up the money I'm hoping to, then yes, there will be a woman."

"Davide told me that we could have a plot of land there just for us, even servants."

Rebecca pulled her knees to her chest. In an instant, she disappeared. She would never come back again.

•

Zoppe touched his head, fingering the folds of the turban that Count Anselmi made him wear.

"Ah, bravo Zoppe, look at you, you're a vision. That blue turban gives you class. My mother, rest her soul, was English, my father, Count Ludovico Anselmi, met her during one of his trips to India. She and her family were in the retinue of the ambassador to the greatest empire on earth. There, my parents admired the class of Indian soldiers with blue turbans."

The British Empire, that's all Count Celestino Anselmi talked about. It was his great obsession.

"Italy deserves one just like it," he went around saying in every drawing room. "We're the ones, after all, who gave the world Augustus. It's up to us to civilize the savages, we're the ones who must bear this heavy burden."

Despite the imperial conceit that made him unpalatable at times, Count Anselmi was the best employer Zoppe could have had in those circumstances.

He was a delicate creature, Count Anselmi, of medium build, with a pearl-gray face. Long hands, thin fingers, ideal for the piano. His straw-colored hair clashed with the dark hair on his arms and his full brown eyebrows. Zoppe suspected that the count manipulated more than one aspect of his body. He was so feminine, polished, evanescent.

It was in Tivoli, at an eighteenth century estate, where the count had received him for the first time two months before.

Zoppe was stunned by all that wealth. Rhinoceros horns and Murano glass, fabrics from Goa and furs from Kazakhstan, Turkish kilims and Persian rugs, miniatures depicting emperors in erotic poses and bound volumes on the holy British Academy.

Next to the rhinoceros horns, Zoppe noticed a stuffed buffalo head. On its face there was almost a sneer of satisfaction.

The room had a pungent odor, like sweaty bodies. Zoppe felt nauseated. Past orgasms and cries of terror resounded in his ears. What had gone on in that house? If he could, he would have run away that instant. But he was no longer free to do anything. The count, with his benevolent air, had bought him. Now Zoppe was his. If he wanted to return to Magalo, if he wanted to see Asha the Rash's beautiful eyes again, he had to get in line.

"Do you know how to dance?" the count asked, starting a pas de deux. "Ah, silly me, you must practice savage dances where you come from." His words had a mix of arrogance and prurience. "Those dances where you're all naked and thrashing around. Like snakes, you know what I mean."

"We don't dance," Zoppe said. "I've never seen anyone in my family dance."

"If affairs of state didn't summon me to higher duties, I'd stay here and dance out my most extreme fantasies. But now I'm thirsty, we need water."

He picked up and rang the bell.

"Teodoro, there you are finally. Bring us a carafe of cold water, I'm dying. Be quick."

The count was pale and not even two glasses of water brought back his color. Zoppe had the impression he was trembling. The count pulled a blue vial out of his pants pocket, brought it to his nose and sniffed hard.

"Listen to me, Zoppe, I pulled you out of trouble because I'm good and you can be of use to me. Show me your tongue."

Zoppe obeyed. By then that was all he knew how to do.

"What a nice, thick, red tongue. Mmm … I like it. It'll be useful in Africa, and if it proves itself, it will be well compensated. Count Anselmi is generous."

16

ADUA

I feel so tired. My face in pieces.

I feel so tired. My eyes swollen. I feel so tired. My back broken.

I want a shower, a pillow, a dream.

But at home my little Titanic is sulking. I don't have the courage to go back. We had a fight, my little elephant.

He and I always got along. Always sweet words between us. Always affectionate. But today this fight, and I'm really not used to it. I'm a softie. I love sinking my hands in my man's spongy, curly hair. I fall asleep there and I feel younger, with more energy.

But today he didn't let me anywhere near his head. "Leave me alone," he said.

He was surly, hostile.

That cowardly boy I saved from the street is now rebelling against me. I should have let him rot on Via Giolitti with that cheap gin he bought from the Bangladeshi for some spare change. Toxic hooch that would have wrecked his arteries and his breath. I should have left him there at Termini station, at the mercy of the elements and the skinheads. At least now I wouldn't have to put up with his sulking.

But my little Titanic is under my protection now. I am his armor. It's my money that protects him from the elements and the skinheads. He has a roof over his head, a belly that's always full, and even time to chitchat with his little friends who have found refuge in Northern Europe. I'm sure he's there all day writing "darling" or "my love." He's glued to Facebook. He sits at the computer spying on the lives of others. And these other people are always young women. Their names are Howa, Halima, Habshiro, Anisa. They live in places where Somalis can count on subsidies and housing on the state's dime. And now that every day my little husband sends his insipid declarations of love to Norway, Finland, Great Britain, Sweden … damned Sweden. I have the impression there's a girl there he really likes. Some Zahra, I think it is. Every time I ask him, "Who are these girls?" he hastily replies, "Cousins."

I've forgiven him these virtual distractions. I know he's going to leave me sooner or later anyway. I know our union is temporary. I'm old, after all. I have skin like a checkerboard and it's not like I feel like having sex all that much at my age. He wants me to take it in my mouth … I feel so dirty telling you … but that's what he wants … and, you know, I try to do it. But I always get horrible neck aches. I do it to make him happy. Plus it's the only thing like that he asks of me. Other than that it's him making me happy. But today he got all sulky and I can't stand it.

You know what we fought about, my little elephant? He saw my movie. Yes, the one movie I made.

It was showing on one of those regional channels with a strange name. He saw the whole thing. From the first frame to the last.

He saw me running naked on the golden sand at Capocotta, he saw when Aldo de Luigi put his hands on my butt, he saw me making out with Nick Tonno in a 1953 Chrysler and he also saw what my privates looked like then. Yes, he saw everything.

Now he has all my kisses and moans imprinted on his mind, and he too was sucked into my headlong expressions of love dubbed at the Via Margutta studio. They gave me a languid, honeyed voice for the movie. "Yours is too harsh," the director told me. Then he added, "If it's dubbed, your sacred body will get the drawl it needs to make every man in the world go head over heels." I nodded like a spring, a forced yes I didn't understand.

Just standing there in front of a movie camera like Rita Hayworth seemed incredible. What mattered was being a diva, the adrenaline, wanting immortality more than anything else.

I wanted to explain to my sweet little Titanic, to my little suckling husband, that I was young then, inexperienced, lost in my celluloid dreams and so alone. I wanted to explain to him what my life was like then. That of course his had been hard, and I understood that it had been difficult to escape from desert marauders and sea junkers, but mine too, as far as difficulty goes, was no joke.

I wanted to tell him how I used to be. How I had imagined my future self. The things I'd wanted for myself when I was younger.

But as usual he didn't let me talk.

He sealed my mouth with his own shouting.

And then he finished with the word sharmutta, whore. My heart was pounding. I was afraid I was going to burst from pain right there in front of that boy.

I pulled myself together and threw a pan at him. Then he started sulking again.

Him judging me. I wanted to strangle him.

17
TALKING-TO

Are you crying, Adua? Do you dishonor me like that? Good girls never cry. Did you see your sister Malika? She didn't even shed one tear, and you, what are you doing now?

Trying to drown me? Did you expect just a tiny cut, Adua? Don't make all this fuss, come on now, you're irritating me. Aunt Fardosa called the best midwife to do your *gudniinka*. Now you're free, Adua, just think about that. You don't have that damned clitoris that makes all women dirty. Snip, it's gone, finally! Thanks be to God. The pain will pass. The pain is momentary. Whereas the joy of this liberation, Adua, endures.

Later, you will have only the happiness of being pure, finally closed as God commands. Your sex won't dangle anymore, Adua. It's beautiful to be pure. A good thing. The best. Think what a nice life you'll have without that nasty knocker hanging obscenely between your legs, as if you were a man. I've seen women with it, and I'll tell you, it's not a pretty sight. They're repulsive, they're hungry for flesh, violent. Noisy. You've been spared, Adua, from this shame. Now you're closed, clean, beautiful. You're like my mother, like my mother's mother, and like all the women worthy of esteem in this big family of ours. Your mother, Asha the Rash, that fool, was against the practice, imagine. She said, "No one will touch my daughter, no one will infibulate her." Luckily she's dead. And now you're saved, closed, without that filthy clitoris reminding you you're a woman. Now nothing will distract you. You'll get a good degree and then I'll give you away to the best of men. When you're older you'll thank me.

18

ZOPPE

Addis Ababa was a puzzle of worlds in a yard of cloth.

Addis was a carnation in bloom, a happy girl, a proud Oromo standing tall. A whore like few others, Addis Ababa.

On the one hand, it kneeled before its emperor; on the other it conspired his ruin.

The city was teeming with spies like never before. Mercenaries, thugs and suspicious faces were everywhere.

Everywhere, signs of war and imminent catastrophe.

"You took your time getting here," said a European who Zoppe gathered was the French owner of the hotel where the count was to take up residence.

The man had a long black mustache and very thick eyebrows. His hooked nose towered over a pink face bloated with wine. He had very long arms and they made Zoppe think of the little octopuses he used to find half-dead on the seashore back in Magalo.

"Pardon my lateness. Africa is so slow," Count Anselmi replied in French, breaking out in boisterous laughter.

The man appreciated the quip and laughed too. "I brought two calashes," he said, interrupting himself.

"We'll put your baggage in the first and you in the second. My donkeys and Arabs will take you all to your destination, à La Douce France."

And with that he whistled at two olive-skinned men with long beards and pristine white *jelabiyad*. "Faruk, Karim, load the gentlemen's luggage."

And then turning to his guests: "Arabs are cheap and they're very efficient, not like those lazy Abyssinians."

Zoppe was not allowed to ride in the carriage. He had to follow on foot, with his own two bundles on his shoulders.

He felt his feet sink with every step. It had just rained and the city was an endless expanse of mud. Zoppe noticed movement in the streets. A strange tumult mixed with the acrid stench of fear. Everywhere were makeshift trenches and military boots riddled with holes.

"There'll be war just like the papers say, you know?" the Frenchman said with a certain enthusiasm. "But the Italians can relax. France won't get in the way of Benito Mussolini's imperial plans. We have Tunisia and they'll get Ethiopia. Seems like a fair deal, wouldn't you say?"

Count Anselmi didn't reply.

He didn't want to reveal himself. He just said, "Oh, Addis Ababa is so cold in the morning, I wasn't expecting that," and shifted the conversation to meteorological matters.

Zoppe looked at the city. Addis Ababa had changed so much since the last time he'd seen it. More modern, angrier in parts.

Addis was so different from Magalo. It was different from Mogadishu too. There was no sea to soothe you and the sky seemed like it was about to squash the residents with its destructive fury. Nature was not kind in Addis Ababa and even the air was hostile. Zoppe felt the cold breath of the highlands hit him square in the face. He shivered. And his eyes teared up. Addis Ababa always put you to the test. But as his father, Haji Safar, always said, that city too, so seemingly detached, had a heart that cradled the dreams of babes on stormy nights. When he was little, his father often dragged him to Addis Ababa. Haji Safar was almost as respected there as in Magalo. People smiled at him on the street and women slipped coffee beans in the wide pockets of his tunic. Haji Safar took those beans and chewed on them with gusto. It was wonderful to see his father's face in those moments. It was a round, full face, so different from his own. Zoppe was thin, long, almost skeletal. And he didn't have his father's proud gait; he limped awkwardly beside him, dragging one foot behind the other through that disgusting swamp.

"I like your servant," the Frenchman said. "First time I've seen a Negro, one of these Somalis, with a blue turban."

"Negros are outlandish, didn't you know?" Count Anselmi replied, giving the Frenchman a knowing wink.

The two Europeans laughed. Zoppe was humiliated.

•

And La Douce France wasn't all that sweet.

It was on a busy street where the nauseating odor of the hides and meats at the nearby market forced the guests to stay in their rooms with the windows closed for most of the morning. Count Anselmi was lucky. His room overlooked a side street where the only smell that came through was the coffee prepared by the neighborhood women. The true loser in the matter was Civa. Nothing but squawks and stink in his room.

Zoppe was arranging, for the umpteenth time in recent days, the young man's belongings in a red trunk when Civa called him with a rather excited "Hey, hey!"

"Sir," Zoppe replied. It bothered him to call him that, but it had been a strict order from Count Anselmi.

"You see that window down there? They say there's one of those ladies down there. You know, those pretty ladies of the night ... the ones ... you know, on the postcards."

"Whores, yes, I know, master."

"Clearly, Zoppe. Don't be so vulgar."

"But sir, that's what they are. I didn't make them take up that trade."

"You're a puritan, Zoppe. A puritan Negro, can you believe the oddities I keep seeing."

Zoppe didn't reply.

Who knows what Haji Safar would have said. His father hadn't appeared in his visions for a while now.

Not even the Limentanis appeared in his dreams anymore. It was as if Addis Ababa and its hectic life had stripped him of all his affections.

Zoppe found himself surrounded by strangers. With no one to confide in.

And since he'd arrived in Addis Ababa his tongue had been infected. It was swollen, sore, and had strange yellow spots on the tip. He'd even spit blood that morning.

He had tried to heal it by chewing the gingerroot he always carried in his pocket. But the infection didn't cease to torment him.

His head hurt too. He couldn't stand the claustrophobic feeling of those overstuffed rooms. That art deco ostentation didn't go well with the armies of termites that attacked European-style furnishings.

Everything was nibbled away. Everything in that strange hotel was half off.

Even the guests.

They were almost all journalists looking for a scoop in that land that would soon be swept up by a colonial war. Mussolini—and it wasn't a secret to anyone—had ordered that the conflict was to begin before German rearmament was completed. If he wanted to attack Ethiopia, the Duce had to do it sometime that year.

Only the journalists had never covered an actual war.

Count Anselmi called them "the circus," and Zoppe couldn't help but agree with his ambiguous master's definition.

Armed with telescopes, first aid kits, tan safari jackets, and gas masks, the circus tried desperately not to appear too ridiculous before the eyes of their own consciences.

They ranged from Communist fans of the Negus to ridiculous Americans in shorts and suspenders. In the morning they met for breakfast with bags under their eyes from bad digestion and cheap alcohol, asking one another: "So what shall we tell our readers today?" They scratched their heads, sipping bitter Ethiopian coffee and looking hopeless. "I can't describe the usual parade of the Ras's warriors, I put that out last week." Someone else in the back of the room: "Luckily in Germany they still go wild over primitive scenes."

"Hey," chimed in one of the rare women in that caravan. "Has anyone ever tried to describe these people's food? They're so caveman-like, they still eat with their hands."

Zoppe, the few times he'd been granted access to the breakfast room, had wondered why those journalists didn't simply tell their readers about the preparations for war.

Addis Ababa was in ferment. The city was fatefully preparing for defense, and every spot, even the holy Cathedral of St. George, had become a trench. In order to keep his people's spirits high, Haile Selassie organized parade after parade. And to show how industrious Ethiopia was, he had foreigners taken around to its hospitals, its prisons, its schools.

"Hey, Zoppe, look." It was Civa calling him back to the present, pointing out the prostitute's window all happy. "She pulled up the curtain, maybe she's free."

"I wouldn't if I were you."

"But ... I'm dying to lie with a beautiful Abyssinian. In Rome I saw certain little photos that got me tempted. They say their cunts are huge and you get lost inside them. Ah, it must be a wonderful sensation," and he began to whistle.

Then suddenly the young woman looked out the window and upon seeing Civa started waving her hands in greeting. She was dressed in white and had an unusual dark veil around her head.

"But ... but ..." Civa stammered.

"That's what I wanted to warn you about. Not what you expected, is it?" "But ... her face ..." the young Italian said, dismayed.

"She's had smallpox. It happens. Accept it. Now get away from there. I think that's been enough of a lesson for today."

Zoppe brusquely lowered the shutters.

19

ADUA

During our history lesson I was called into the headmaster's office.

That had never happened before.

I hadn't done anything wrong, at least not that I could recall.

It was a hot day in 1976. I think it was November. In Magalo, the sun blazed. Rain, a distant memory. "There will be terrible shortages," the elders said. My legs trembled.

Drops of sweat beaded on my oval face. I looked right at the headmaster. A plea in my eyes: "Be quick." But the headmaster didn't speak, he just looked at me and shook his head. Then he began fiddling with a pen and paper. He made a few doodles. I didn't look away, it was as if I was frozen. I was supposed to look at the floor, show more humility. But my eyes locked with his. He had strange green eyes. I held my breath.

"Your father has been arrested," he said solemnly. I looked down. Now there was really no sense in staring at the headmaster. I didn't want to see the expression of triumph on his face. The headmaster hated my father. All the men in Siad Barre's new regime did.

My father didn't hide his aversion to the dictator or to the new direction Somali politics had taken. "These Communists will lead us to ruin," he kept saying. Hajiedda Fardosa begged him to keep quiet. But he continued to speak out. "Trash," he'd say, and let out a big wad of spit in demonstration of all his contempt.

"Don't you think of your daughters?" Hajiedda Fardosa asked him. "Don't you think about their future? They'll be the ones to pay if you keep acting this way."

"They can handle it. They're big now. I can't think about them. It's my conscience."

I'd been expecting the arrest. We all had. I stood there, silent, waiting to be dismissed. But the headmaster didn't let me go. He kept playing with his pen, with his doodles.

"Your father," he said, again breaking the bitter silence, "has been accused of insubordination. It's a very serious charge." I nodded, tired of the bad comedy. "Nothing to say?"

I was berated, and I quickly mustered: "Yes, Headmaster, it's a very serious charge." What was I supposed to do? Apologize? Kneel at his feet? Did he expect me to tear my hair out? What did he want? Then he looked at me with his unmoving eyes, black and empty.

"I'll be keeping an eye on you. You know what they say, like father, like daughter." I was dismissed and I returned to class. No one asked me why the headmaster had called me in. No one talked to me after class, not even Muna Kinky-Hair, my dearest friend at the time. Not even you, Muna, will talk to me anymore? You, who have been outcast by everybody because you're a nappy-headed *jeerer*? You, who are considered to be from a lower caste, a Bantu Somali with a big nose and wide backside? Even you, Muna, would betray me like that? I had suddenly become a pariah. Someone to avoid.

When I got back home, there was Hajiedda Fardosa with a face more glum than usual and yellow cheeks that clearly attested to the failing state of her liver. "We can see him this afternoon," she told me. Malika didn't come along. She wasn't well. She had thrown up, unable to take the news. I didn't feel sorry for her. You could never count on Malika, not even in a time of need.

The temporary detention center was in the Affissione Est district. Far from home. Hajiedda Fardosa and I walked for kilometers between twigs and hot sand. There was no sea there. The landscape was dominated by the lunar solitude of the African periphery. It went through your eyes and affronted your heart. Once we arrived we waited at a green gate for an hour. Hajiedda Fardosa had sandy feet and dirty nails. I stood off to the side with my legs crossed. I looked at my hands. I was harboring the biggest of secrets. The week before, thanks to Omar Genale, I had met some Italians. Omar Genale. What a character! He was fat when no one else in Somalia was. Now everyone is fat, especially those of us in the diaspora like me. They drown their homesickness in heaps of mustard and fried meat. But during my teenage years, Omar was the only fat one in the city. He had a pointy mustache, a flat chin, piggish eyes and sweet little dimples like a baby Jesus. He always had a bunch of smiles handy, especially "for big beauties like you, Adua." The prematurely aged child really made me laugh. His walk, I remember, was especially funny. He scampered on his toes like a rabbit. But his was a hop full of fat, a tired hop from the notable bulk of flab that he was carrying.

Omar trafficked in all sorts of items. You wanted butter and he had it brought directly from Nairobi. French cigarettes, there they were. Italian magazines, no need to even ask. Housewives relied on him for flour. And big beauties like me asked him for contraband cassette tapes. Gianni Morandi, Jackson 5, Stevie Wonder, Omar had everything. He knew how to navigate the intricate network of illegal trade. No one imagined that such a big, heavy man could go as light as a dragonfly between the narrow clefts of a despotic regime. He was good at his job, Omar. It wasn't particularly commendable, but it was what a depleted city like Magalo needed. "Good job, Omar," the Italians told him. "You brought us the right girl." Someone else in the group: "She has nice legs, this Negro girl." Naturally he was compensated. And he was given the task of taking me to the airport on the agreed-upon date. "Bring her to us; the rest, the exit documents, we'll take care of that." And so the deal was sealed. More money was promised to Omar Genale. And I literally felt like I was in seventh heaven. They were Italian, they wanted to make movies, they would turn me into a Marilyn and I'd leave that sewer Magalo forever.

But now I was standing at a green gate with my legs crossed waiting to visit my arrested father in jail. Italy was still too far away. A strong wind began to ruffle our clothes. Sand blew into our eyes, Hajiedda Fardosa teared up. I squeezed my eyes shut as hard as I could. Meanwhile, my mind wandered. What would I say to him once we were inside? We never talked. What did he expect me to do? I didn't know how to love him.

And he didn't know how to love me. And meanwhile, the wind kept pounding us. It hit hard.

I squeezed my eyes shut again. When they opened the green gate I almost didn't notice. Hajiedda Fardosa tugged me and I straightened up like a newly bloomed flower. In front of me was a man in uniform but without a hat. He wore glasses. He said nothing. He motioned for us to follow him. The man was bald. He had a large, pockmarked face. A cruel face I could have gladly done without. He put his hands on my bottom. I looked toward Hajiedda Fardosa for support, but she was looking the other way. Blood shot to my brain. I wrung my hands. Luckily, I thought, I was about to leave all this behind. In three days I'll be out of here. I already pictured myself in Rome, a city I knew from books. In my head I recited the names of its streets and its squares: Via Sistina, Via Giulia, Piazza di Spagna, Piazza Navona, Via Veneto … How wonderful! I already saw myself wrapped in a black Givenchy dress like Audrey Hepburn, ready to climb the ladder to success. The Italians liked me. They were going to have me make a movie.

They would make me immortal. No more Magalo, no more troubles, no more headmasters calling me or best friends betraying me.

Hajiedda Fardosa and I were led into a room with turd-colored walls. The police officer escorting us said "Wait here," and then shot me a nasty, mean look. It didn't register. My imagination was elsewhere. I was in Rome, on Via Margutta, on Via del Corso. Then a man in a trapezoidal green uniform appeared. He introduced himself as the director of the institution. He was nicer than the policeman, less vulgar. He had a translucent mustache that put anyone around him in a good mood. "He's a stubborn one, your husband," the director told Hajiedda Fardosa. "Talk some sense into him and he'll be out of here soon."

"I'll try," Hajiedda Fardosa said, biting her lip.

Then Papa was brought in.

He was smiling, in contrast to the atmosphere in that turd-colored room. The blue turban he always wore was sloppily wrapped. My father was thinner. His eyes more intense. He seemed happy. Satisfied. I looked at Hajiedda Fardosa. She hadn't expected that smile either. I wanted to kiss him on the cheek. I'd never done it before. How does one kiss one's father? No one ever taught me. No one touched at home. Let alone kissed. I took a step toward him. I reached out. I should at least shake his hand. A manly gesture, one that he would understand. I took one step, two, three—then I tripped over a chair I hadn't noticed. I fell flat on my face. A ridiculous fall. Like in a silent film, something out of Charlie Chaplin, Buster Keaton.

Everyone laughed and the tension melted. "I have a clumsy daughter," my father said.

20

TALKING·TO

I can't stand you looking at me like that, Adua, like you're scolding me. I'm the father. You're just the daughter. I can look at you that way, you can't. You're nobody. Without me you wouldn't have even been born. These are things you would do better not to forget. And I'm sick of these questions about your mother. What do you want to know? You mention her all the time, muttering to yourself. You think I don't see you trying to talk with the shadow of that woman? You never even met Asha the Rash. You don't even know what her face was like. And you dare talk to her? Adua, what are you talking to her for? You're pathetic sometimes. I'm not a fool or blind. I see everything you do. But that woman, no, that whore, don't mention her name in my presence again. She chose to die, she left us. Don't mention her, ever. And even if you've gotten big I can still beat you till your soul bleeds. Don't take advantage of my good heart. I haven't beaten you for years and I have no intention to start again now. But stop bringing her up. That woman is nothing. Just a mistake.

21

ZOPPE

Citrons didn't break. They weren't weak like the fragile papayas or soft mangos. Citrons were warriors, their cores made of metal and their pulp was as if covered in armor. It was a strange alchemy that kept citrons alive. The sweet soul was in fact a defense against a rough, thick skin. That's what guaranteed the heavenly fruit a quiet life without any trouble. Citrons were more resistant than lemons, harder than grapefruits. Ideal for target practice.

"You'll see, brother, they're just what we've been looking for."

Semeon was enthusiastic about his discovery. And he wouldn't stop singing its praises. To him, those rough citruses had the advantage of being not too small, but not gigantic either. They were what Semeon called "the ideal size."

"I saw them at the market, down at Tessa's. They're just right for us, my brother, they're perfect. Shooting at them will be like shooting right at the temple of the Italian enemy," Semeon told him the first time.

And since then, Dagmawi had taken up the habit of going outside the city to the big clearing with a big basket full of citrons.

A basket, and a weapon hidden under his arm.

That fruit had become the center of his existence. On the horizon, a future as a warrior.

Normally he went alone to the clearing. His Somali friend Zoppe had come to see him. What a treat! He really needed someone to share his troubles with. Since he'd started training, he was suffering. It was as if something were eating him from the inside out. It was nice for once to have some company, not to go down that long thorny road in solitude.

It had been five years since they'd seen each other last. In those five years they had become men. In those five years the responsibilities had piled up on their shoulders.

Zoppe sported a nice Sufi beard, though his hands remained as soft as a young girl's. They were hands that had never seen soil or the hard labor of that daily back-and-forth. Dagmawi, on the other hand, knew all about it. He had been working at the Indian emporium Mohamedally for three years, and by now his life was organized by the packages he had to load and unload. Flour, rice, curry, chili pepper, cumin, as well as hides, meats, beans, eggs.

He worked hard at Mohamedally, and from the labor his once smooth hands were covered with little wrinkles of suffering.

But Zoppe suffered too. You could see it in his furrowed brow and his constantly quivering shoulders.

Dagmawi wanted to ask his friend the reason for all his anxiety, but decided to wait.

Once they reached the clearing they would tell each other everything.

"It'll seem crazy to you, Zoppe, my friend," he said, almost anticipating the confession, "but these citrons are the best thing that have happened to me in the last six months, at least … yes, definitely the best. All I have left to keep me from going crazy are the citrons. Zoppe, will I be capable of killing?"

Zoppe didn't breathe a word. He just took a citron and bounced it off his right hand.

"What about your marriage? Since you wrote me you've been married for about five months … Is it possible that these citrons are better than your woman?"

"Yes," Dagmawi said curtly.

He loved Tezetà, his wife, but those citrons … ah, those citrons … they were the corollary of something bigger, more absolute.

Those citrons were the tangible proof of a man's love for his land.

·

Zoppe had already forgotten the citrons. His soul had taken him back to the vision he'd seen at dawn, several hours before.

He'd barely slept that night. The cries of a wounded dog in the distance kept him awake.

He had asked Count Anselmi for the day off and strangely the count put up no resistance.

"I know you're not going to run away anyway. You can't. So go ahead and enjoy a day of complete leisure." And then, with a coy wink, continued: "The body's needs must be satisfied. These little Ethiopian girls are like good wine from the hills, all it takes is a couple of glasses to tide you over for the next ten years."

No point in explaining to the lecherous count that he wasn't going to see a woman. Not that he didn't miss a woman's sweet breath … At home, as soon as he got back, he would find Asha the Rash waiting for him. He loved Asha. He had promised himself, under the shade of a sycamore, that he would make her his. And Zoppe was a man of his word.

He missed his future bride. A woman with a big backside and a contagious laugh.

Asha the Rash, *afar indhood* as the neighbors called her, because of the thick tortoiseshell spectacles a Turkish doctor had advised her to wear.

But that morning, the thought of Asha was swept away by a vision. A bad vision.

The contours of the world were jagged and opaque. His eyes teared up. His mouth suddenly went dry. And his tongue became stiff, lifeless.

The vision came before he left the hotel. He saw wood huts burning. He recognized that place. He'd been there with Haji Safar on one of his trips. His father would go there to heal children from their demons. That was how he met Dagmawi and his family. His father had cured a friend of his from the evil eye. And since then the two boys had been inseparable. Haji Safar loved that town, loved those people. "Here was once the kingdom of Bilqis, the one the *gaal* call the Queen of Sheba. If we exist in this world, my son, it is because of her. That is why I often come to this foreign land. I reunite with the spirit of the ancient queen." Haji Safar loved that land, and he was delighted to be able to give a little hope to those people without a future. There, among the poor, East Africa overcame its differences. There, all divisions were canceled out. Zoppe could have recognized that big district out of a thousand. How much time he had spent there as a little boy, romping in the mud with Dagmawi and little Semeon. The area was between Sidist Kilo and the old market. There, his father was respected and venerated. Seeing those huts burning was an immense horror for Zoppe, who collapsed in the doorway like a rag. In the vision, everything was being set on fire. He saw brown uniforms, taut cheekbones, onion-shaped eyes, pink skin, black corpses.

Then the vision, just as it came, vanished into air.

It dissipated with the first morning light, without leaving a trace, except in his human heart.

·

"This is the clearing, dear Zoppe. We're here," Dagmawi said.

Just then a treacherous wind began bellowing from the west.

In an instant Zoppe's skin became hard and bluish. Everything was flat and empty. A few shrubs here and there. A few solitary animals.

The citrons in that lunar landscape truly looked heavenly.

Dagmawi took one in his hand. It was yellow, oval and had a slight bump at the peduncle. He touched it. He almost shivered. It was so much like a woman's nipple.

The man began to play with the citron, rolling it from one hand to the other. A frozen expression on his face. He was talking to the citron, coaxing it. He wanted to understand its most recondite secrets, suck out its wisdom before destroying it. Then he gripped it decisively and threw it into the distance. "Nice curve," Zoppe yelled. But Dagmawi didn't hear him, Dagmawi was shooting.

A suffocating silence muffled the eardrums like silk. There were only the citrons and their unrelenting thirst for vengeance. Everything was deadened and soft. Only the flapping wings of the horrible marabous clashed with the clouds in the sky. They were shrieking over some carcass they'd scented nearby.

Dagmawi didn't like marabous. They were a bad omen. He had seen many of them during work. Sometimes he came across a load of spoiled meat and it was his job to carry it as far away as possible from the emporium. Those beasts waited for the meat to rot, and when the first worms came out of the carcass, they would swoop down onto what had once been alive. Nothing scared them, not even his presence, not even his pitchfork.

Dagmawi looked at Zoppe. "When I have real bombs in my hand, will I be so brave?"

"Maybe," Zoppe replied, doubtful.

"The Italians are going to crush us, aren't they?" Dagmawi insisted.

"They have modern weapons," Zoppe said noncommittally.

To distract himself, Zoppe picked up a citron too. It was round, shiny, inviting like few other things in this world. The citron reminded him of his Asha's curves. He started peeling it. Slowly. Then he ate it.

22

ADUA

"You don't dress well."

So the boy whose mouth I feed said to me this morning.

I should say, "So my husband said to me," but as the days go by I feel he's less and less of a husband and more of a burden.

I can't seem to care about him or respect him like I used to. Besides, he doesn't love me anymore either. He didn't love me when we got married, to tell the truth, but at least he was kind, considerate. The rascal always knew what to do with a fool like me. He played the part of the chivalrous knight perfectly and I melted at his fake declarations of love. I knew—because I'm not dumb—that he was never motivated by genuine feelings for me. It was clear what attracted him was having a place to sleep, the hot soup I offered him, more than my long-faded graces. But despite it all, I accepted that fiction, because it was the only thing in the world that still gave me a little warmth, a jolt of life. With him I realized at least in part my ridiculous childhood dreams. That's why I pretended to believe him—I did it for that little girl from the past—and in that vulnerable state jumped into his arms like a freezing little animal. To his credit, the little bastard has always known how to handle me, he was always good at that. Not by chance did he pretend to be more in love than anyone else, the most devoted of the devoted. His eyes were so funny and false. So cheerful and deceitful. I laughed at his efforts, but deep down I was also a little flattered. Like a good master, I liked to see him kneel at my feet and ask for just a few crumbs of love in return. As a magnanimous mistress I threw him what little he needed in order to adore me. Not one ounce more or less. I was good at measuring out my power, or what, poor stupid me, I thought was power. And he was good at being falsely devoted to me. There were days, especially the ones streaked with gray lines and bad omens, when he greeted me with a brilliant smile, and if he saw I was especially tired he happily massaged my aching feet.

Sometimes he sang me songs full of love. "For my beauty, for my darling," he said.

He would make paper flowers to frame my pretty little face.

I laughed at these sentimentalities. I found all that teenage romanticism ridiculous, those rose-colored thoughts that weren't for me. And if I think about it, they weren't for him either. Since when did two Somalis, especially ones with nomadic backgrounds like us, give each other treacle-colored flowers?

We who had known hunger, separation, suffering—what the hell were we supposed to do with a flower?

I told him so.

Flowers weren't part of our culture; he should stop with these Western affectations copied from who knows where.

I was harsh, so that he would be even sweeter with me. I wanted him to soften all my asperities, cradle my wounded self, compensate for my cultural maladjustments.

Usually he did. But sometimes what I also heard out of his little viper mouth was a truth I wasn't ready to hear.

Once, I don't remember now if it was in the morning or afternoon, he asked me: "When you were young, you never loved anyone, did you Adua?" His face was completely serious. It scared me.

I remember looking at him a little taken aback, a little offended. How dare he judge me, this kid? How dare he hurt me with his pointed words? Had he perhaps forgotten that I had been the one to take him off the street and feed him?

What did that peach-fuzzed little boy know about my youth? What did he know about how much suffering I'd buried in my chest?

I closed myself in a dome of silence. Pissed. Furious. But it didn't last long. I can never really stay mad at him. Usually it takes just one of his little quirks to put a bright big smile back on my face.

And that was when he, like a perfect Lancelot, would get down on one knee before me and with hands joined on his chest, start to recite the love poems that his poor paralytic mother had taught him one night to distract him from the bombs falling like hailstones over their bare heads. It was *jidaal*, the season that brings nothing and spares nothing, but the little boy's heart filled up with his mother's chimeras as fast as a wineskin.

Ah, how I loved those poems where valiant camel riders saved maidens on the pasture from the insatiable ferocity of the hyenas. I saw myself in every girl and my heart beat with every heart.

"Recite, recite some more, little one," I commanded. And with his clear and sonorous voice from better days he transported me to a time before all time, where not even dreams yet had a home.

Now however, none of this happened any more between us. That debauched Titanic is sprawled out in front of the TV almost all day long.

I wonder when he's going to leave me.

At this point I don't wonder *if* anymore, but more realistically, *when*. We barely touch at all anymore.

I think he's had enough of my barren womb.

His every cell, I can feel it, is pushing him forcefully to make an heir for himself.

Today I wondered whether the "You don't dress well" which he shouted cruelly in my face was none other than the beginning of our end.

How ironic. Radiant me, today I'm dressed like a housemaid.

I remember when I was young I brought the sun to Italy, to this crater of illusions that swallowed me up.

It was the twentieth century and I was the most beautiful in the land.

Arturo Sposetti, the director of the film I starred in as the *Femina Somala*, box office smash in the year of grace 1977, always told me I was the most beautiful. Arturo had a big paunch that didn't match his little arms, as slender as a rachitic boy's. No hair on his face. Smooth as a young girl. He looked like a hippopotamus, with that sleepy air he had. He smoked a pipe. I remember how much I liked smelling the pungent odor of tobacco when he was nearby. He rarely laughed. He squinted like a sloth. And for every little thing he'd slap me on the rear like a sailor. But he did it listlessly. He contorted himself to fit the masculine role which destiny had affixed onto him. Everything about his gestures betrayed little conviction.

And it seemed like life didn't interest him all that much. He'd get excited about my Somali fabrics, though. He went crazy over my tunics.

"That dress you're wearing is magnificent. I want it on the movie poster," he told me, with that hollow smile of his.

And sure enough I'm wearing a Somali tunic on the poster, though it's carefully cropped, almost up to my groin, to leave my legs exposed.

And to make the whole thing look even more savage Arturo had me take the photo perched on a big plastic baobab like Jane from *Tarzan*.

The idea for the tree was Sissi's. She had all the extravagant ideas.

ADUA

And in fact it was Sissi, Arturo's wife, who had chosen me for the movie.

"She was the one who wanted you. And in general she was the one who insisted on having a Somali."

They'd forked over quite a bit to get me a passport, a visa, an airline ticket. And Somali customs authorities didn't look twice. Sissi wanted me at all costs. But in the end I cost the production very little. I thanked them by running away from home with my best fabrics.

I didn't say good-bye to anyone, not even Muna Kinky-Hair, my ex-friend. I was too afraid of last minute revelations. I didn't want to get caught by an enraged father and his sympathetic community. So in silence I let myself be swallowed up by an Alitalia Boeing with a stopover in Addis Ababa.

"She's gonna make us rich, this Negress," and to celebrate, they sang *"Faccetta Nera"* on the airplane—the 1930s fascist anthem about an Abyssinian girl being taken to Rome after the invasion of Ethiopia. They sang it to me a hundred times, shaking my long arms, asleep from the weight of my runaway's pack.

"During the African campaign my father bought a wife from where you're from," Sissi told me that first night on the plane. I just nodded, waiting for the rest of a story that never came.

Sissi never mentioned her father again.

In general, the Sposettis didn't talk much.

They didn't tell me much about the movie, to tell the

truth. I knew only that the main character was called Elo and that she was a photographer.

"So when can I read the script?" I asked.

I wasn't illiterate and I couldn't wait to read that script. But no, they didn't give anything away.

And that is how for several days, weeks even, I lived in ignorance. Elo ... who are you, Elo?

Yaad tahay?

I wondered what sort of face I'd give her. What tone of voice. What bearing, what gestures.

No one had told me yet that Elo undressed completely and gave herself away to men like a dog in heat.

Then one night Arturo and Sissi told me everything. And they told me crudely. It was May. Yes, May.

It was a freezing night, a strangely freezing night for springtime in Italy. I was dressed too lightly for the occasion. I was wearing a tunic because Sissi had insisted so much, because she'd told me, "You have to be extra beautiful for us tonight." A delicate scarf covered my bare shoulders lightly. I was shivering with cold, but I tried not to let it show too much. We were in a seaside town near Rome, I don't remember which; the boardwalk was empty and the pizzeria we had come out of was closing. An insidious wind ruffled our exposed souls and a strange light flashed in a distant window.

"What a moon tonight, look," Arturo said, turning to his wife.

She didn't reply. She just said: "Why don't you take us

to the beach house? That way Adua can see it."

I was tired. I wanted to jump in bed and sleep, close my eyes and sleep for a century or two. But Sissi terrified me and so I faked enthusiasm.

Sissi, I realize now that some time has passed, had a cunning beauty that could stop a too fragile heart like mine. Not because she was beautiful, but because there was this need for control in her that was difficult to get away from. That night her bobbed hair was tousled, she wore a casual blouse, a pair of jeans, a burst of beads and leather laces that wrapped around her big feet. Her face shone with an intense light and her salt-and-pepper hair accented the intense green of her almond eyes.

Her nose was straight, her build robust, her chest abundant, but despite her bulk she wasn't a fat person. Her hands were big, though her shoulders were oddly tiny. I noted with an expert eye that she regulated this flaw with modest shoulder pads, which gave a certain consistency to all her bodily contradictions.

It was she who asked me: "Are you bored?"

"No, dear," I said, in the meek voice I had back then.

"Good," she said, relieved. "We have a nice surprise for you."

Arturo, meanwhile, didn't speak. He wasn't a man of many words. He usually grumbled and when he wasn't busy grumbling he was smoking his pipe.

When we got to the beach house, they offered me a scotch. "I don't drink," I said. It was true.

"A drop won't do you any harm, it's a party." I was struck again by that fear. Sissi's voice chilled my soul. I didn't have the strength to tell her no. I drank.

And that sly pair gave me all sorts of things. Vodka, whisky, wine, gin. Mixing in excessive amounts.

Soon I was drunk.

And I, who didn't know how to say no to the people I considered my benefactors, knocked back one after another, with an idiotic smile on my face.

"They took me away from that pit Magalo, they're having me make a movie like Marilyn, they care about me." That's what I thought then.

And the more I wanted to say no, the more I knocked back those obscene concoctions because my head refused to let go of the idea of Elo, who was going to make me famous like Marilyn.

"If you leave, they'll give the part to someone else," my head told me, as I contemplated every tolerable sacrifice to be Marilyn.

I knew they were after my body. I wasn't that naïve.

I knew sooner or later I would have to pay that tax. A friend had warned me. "They'll ask for your body. That's what the Italians did with my grandmother. I don't think these ones are any different, you know? You just have to figure out if you are willing to pay the price or not."

I would have paid anything to become Marilyn. Or at least that's what I thought then.

I didn't know that they would take everything from me. Even my dignity. I let myself be touched, groped, smelled.

Their hands were frenzied, their breath heavy. She gave the orders, and he followed them.

Then she kissed him and he squeezed my tits. It went on and on. I felt like one big bruise.

"We're teaching you, Adua," Sissi told me at one point, when I was on the verge of passing out from exhaustion and alcohol.

"Teaching me?" I said.

"You'll have to do this in the movie."

"In the movie?"

"You're awkward. Hesitant. We've studied you. You've never been touched by a man, have you, Adua?"

I was plastered. I couldn't even respond. I wanted to scream. But I was too weak. Too weak. I wonder if this had happened to Marilyn too.

Marilyn, so sweet and so jaded. Urban legend had it that once she got a star on her dressing room door she exclaimed, laughing indecorously: "Now I'll only do it with the ones I want to." No more fellatio to land an audition, no more quickies in the elevator to reach a certain director.

Marilyn had earned her place in the star system. And me?

Would I have the guts to go from fellatio to fellatio to reach my dream? I didn't know what my answer was. I was too drunk.

And that was when, as I was lost in my thoughts, she ordered him: "Now undress her, Arturo!" He looked at me sidelong, hollowly embarrassed, and with a flick undid the tie on my tunic.

And for the first time I was naked in front of my director.

"Arturo, she's yours, do whatever you want with her," Sissi said in a hard military voice that froze my blood. And that was when Arturo noticed the stitches.

"This one is all closed up down there," he told his wife. "Closed?"

"Yeah, it's like she's run through with barbed wire."

"What are you talking about, Arturo?" And she too, who had mostly limited herself to giving orders from the feather couch, jumped up on the bed, all disheveled, to see the strange barbed wire that their Somali girl had in that so delicate spot.

"Adua, what did they do to you down there?" I didn't respond. I was so sleepy. "Answer, you twit. What did they do to you down here?" I didn't respond. I didn't have the strength.

I barely heard their words.

That's when Sissi slapped me, one, two, three times. "Listen, I repeat, what did they do to you down there, fool?"

And that's when I said: "They do it to all the girls in my country. They cut our *siil*, the part that hangs down. They cut off other stuff down there too. Of course it hurts, but then you get a bunch of gifts and it's nice. I got a shell. Then they sew us up. That way we remain pure, we're virgins, and we stay that way until our wedding day, when someone loves us and opens us up with his love," I replied with a whimper.

"Love?" she rebuked. "What a useless word."

"You don't need love, stupid. We can open you up with a pair of scissors. And then finally Arturo will be able to taste you."

Scissors?

Did she say scissors?

I tried to wriggle away … to beg them. But there were two of them, they were stronger than me, and also more lucid.

And that's how on that strange May night I was deflowered by a pair of scissors. I wonder if the same thing happened to Marilyn.

I wonder …

23
TALKING-TO

Where did you find that picture? Do you look through my stuff, Adua? And what do you mean you want an explanation?

I won't give you any explanation and I won't tell you who those white people in the photo are either. I can tell what you're trying to do.

I realize that you doubt my being a patriot and a nationalist. You think I'm acting.

Your mother thought the same thing. Always questioning me, not taking me at my word. It's like I can still hear your silly mother. "Dear, why don't you tell me the truth? Everyone worked with the whites during that time anyway." She thought I was a traitor, a bad person. She didn't love me, your mother. She thought the worst of me. And then she would whine and beg for some truth and it bothered me so much when she said it was all the same to her, it didn't matter. How could it not matter? There's a big difference between betraying your country and fighting for it. But then your mother said "I love you" and to her those words settled everything. She was a silly goose, a dupe, a fool. And headstrong too. Always sitting there asking me about my past, the whites, the wars I went through.

She was a nosy pain in the neck. And now you're doing the same thing? You women, you're impossible. Creatures from hell. I can't stand you.

24
ZOPPE

The man had kind eyes, a long beard and big ears like an elephant's.

The man was bent over big sheets of paper all day. He spent hours sketching the world. He drew trees, butterflies, gnats, girls. His realm was the courtyard of the Hotel La Douce France; he wasn't interested in touring like the other guests. There was no agitation in his movements. Zoppe envied him. He too would have liked to sit there doing nothing. Instead he had to run all over Addis Ababa with Count Anselmi. Lately, their days had become frenetic. And Zoppe's tongue had dried up in his throat from translating. He translated, but he lost the sense of the words. It was as if his thoughts were floating away from him in a storm cloud. But the count had fallen ill that day. "My head is spinning," he'd said that morning. "I hope it's not a fever; I'm going to lie down for a while." Zoppe was pleased. He couldn't stand any more running around muddy Addis in his old shoes and he hoped the fever would last as long as possible. That's how he found himself in the courtyard with the elephant-eared man that strange morning.

He looked at him as if for the first time.

There was something so familiar in the figure bent over the sketch paper. As if they'd already met. His skin was a little yellow. Covered with strange brown spots and a thick layer of pink dust that Zoppe couldn't quite explain. He couldn't figure out where the strange man came from either. It was like he had emerged from the depths of some crater. There was something ancient about him and at the same time familiar.

The man looked at him and then said in a language that he knew very well: "I'd like to draw a portrait of you."

What to do?

Zoppe knew in his heart that he had to dodge the request. He had to say "No, thanks." "No, I don't feel like it." "No, you frighten me." "No, I don't want you to."

Instead he said yes.

He couldn't resist the kindness of those familiar-seeming eyes.

.

After three hours, the drawing was finished. "Can I see it?" Zoppe asked.

"I would rather you not."

"But … but what do you mean? I sat here without moving for three hours for you."

"The drawing will hurt you."

"Let me be the judge of that, damn it," Zoppe said in an arrogant tone he'd never before used in his life.

The man motioned for him to come closer. Zoppe looked. Then, he fainted.

•

That night he dreamed of the drawing. On one side, there was a man with a blue turban, his face disfigured by an egg-shaped scar that made him look strangely fierce. He was throwing a javelin. His arms were muscular. His movements coordinated. He was almost handsome in that athletic pose. On the other side was an elephant. Big ears, a big trunk. The elephant resembled him in a way too. The elephant knew the javelin was aiming his way. Zoppe noted something in the animal's eyes. Something that he knew well. It was called terror.

•

He didn't find anyone sitting under the baobab at La Douce France. The yellowish man had disappeared. He asked the other servants if they had seen him. No one knew anything about it. A young man named Hamid, originally from Harar, told him: "There was no man sitting under that baobab. Yesterday it was just you sitting there, nobody else. You dreamed that man up, my friend."

•

That night Zoppe remembered the words of his Aunt Bibi, the soothsayer. "Our conscience," she used to say, "has a face."

•

That's how Zoppe ended up sitting on the bed with his legs folded waiting for something to happen.

The yellowish man didn't take long to come.

He still had elephant ears. But his skin was darker, grainier.

"I don't understand," Zoppe blurted out, confused. "Who in the devil are you?"

"I'm you. How can you not recognize me? How can you still be confused?"

Only then did Zoppe remember that he had ears like an elephant's and his skin had spots. He also remembered that he drew when he was upset. Putting lines and curves on paper had always helped him calm down. Whatever he didn't understand, he drew. That yellowish man was his conscience taking bodily form. As his Aunt Bibi had always said: "Our conscience has a face."

25
ADUA

I'm naked …

Sand covering me like gold …

Up in a tree waiting to be devoured …

Big lips slicked with gloss for extra allure … Eyebrows furrowed, like a cat, well defined …

Kohl highlighting my eyes, and who knows, maybe even my desire … Bangs straightened by a flesh-eating iron …

Brightly colored wraps in the beach scenes … A little hairspray and I feel effervescent … And beads all over my body …

Lying back on calfskin I display myself obscenely to an oblivious world. Meanwhile he's hollering, "Close your legs more baby, don't show the hair, not yet, save it for now." And a moment later, "Now fling them open, like the windows when you wake up in the morning." He has a raspy, cavernous voice. He scares me. He's the director of my movie, though. He's my master, he bought me for peanuts at a sale down in East Africa. I can't contradict him. So I nod, obedient, passive, as befits the defenseless like me.

My nails are sharp as the claws of a proud lioness.

The manicurist told me, "With these, no one can break you."

Didn't she have the experience to know that the nails of small-time starlets don't last?

She should know that better than anyone.

My nails will break, milady. And sometimes my heart breaks too. I scratch, bite, paw.

But it all lasts an instant. Time for one take. For one regret.

"Give me languid now, baby," the director orders.

"Move those hips, come on, be a good girl."

And I am a good girl. Because that's my job as an actress. I'm a professional, I think.

I wallow in that fiction.

"Now move your wrists in circles … that's good, like an odalisque in the pasha's harem. Let the dance take you over, baby, and then move over to him nice and slow, you're a panther, baby, remember that. And now kiss him, yeah, kiss him with passion."

Armando smells like garlic, but I have to pretend to love him, pretend that he's my only reason for living.

I move toward him and smell vodka. But I know the script says I'm supposed to claw him like a little kitten. I follow orders like a cadet. I have no other choice. It's written in the script. He lowers my head, authoritative.

"See how good I am? Not one complaint, boss," I say to the director. But no one answers me now.

Has the set been taken down? Where am I?

And where's my movie?

Who are you, man who reeks of vodka? And what is this mahogany furniture around us?

Where's the tropical beach we re-created at Capocotta with fake palm trees? Where's the crew? And my makeup artist? That fat lady who cleans me off and wipes my sweat every other second? And those maniacal costumers checking every wrinkle on my skimpy little dress?

Where on earth has everyone gone?

I'm still wearing my costume. I'm still made up like a slut.

But then I remember, everything comes back to me in a jolt of pain.

I'm not on the set anymore. We wrapped at five. They've taken me to a luxury villa in the middle of Rome, off of a famous piazza.

It was Sissi, it's always her, always that disaster of a woman, who told me in her fake nunnish tone: "There's a dinner at the distributor's house, you know, that magnate who gave us all that money for the movie … he invited us. He wants to see you."

And I, dismissive, said: "Me?" I remember always having had that sharp tone of voice with Sissi. Essentially, I couldn't forgive her for what she'd done to me.

"So basically you have to go and you have to play nice with him."

"Nice?" I asked, a little disconcerted.

"Do you want to become a star or not? Well you've got

to play nice, honey, otherwise you can forget about being a star."

"Forget about it?"

"Yes, honey. And put on a nice little dress, it's an elegant dinner."

"Really elegant?"

"Just the right amount, you'll see."

It was almost all women at the party, all with skimpy rags barely covering our privates. And we all had plastic smiles contorting our faces.

We were brunettes, blondes, redheads, one with purple hair—"She's eccentric," someone whispered to me. They'd also recruited an Asian, maybe Japanese or Korean, and then of course there was me, the drop of chocolate over the double layer of whipped cream.

He came up to me and said: "So you're Arturo's Negress. Not bad. Long legs. I like the ones with long legs."

I looked at Sissi. I was alarmed. I felt so dirty. So empty.

Sissi pushed me toward him and said: "He'll give you orders like Arturo on the set, you follow them, piece of cake."

I go down a long hallway with that man, who barely came up to my shoulder blades. He keeps his hand on my bottom, kind of like Arturo during the first days of shooting.

"How old are you?" the magnate asks.

"Twenty," I lie.

"A round number, like all of them, of age then … the

others always are too." And after a low laugh, he adds: "Between us, it's smart not to say seventeen, seventeen is bad luck," and gives me a conspiratorial wink.

I don't know what to say. I nod just to do something.

"Put this on, go over there," he orders.

It's a nurse costume. I don't understand what it's for. But I put it on, without a word. I don't feel like contradicting the bald man with halitosis.

"But don't put anything underneath. I like bare skin." I obey.

And then without much of a prelude he has me kneel down in front of him. "Afterward I'll introduce you to the guests as the cousin of some sheikh."

And with that, he pulls my hair back and looks at me, hurting me, and then pushes me towards his nether parts.

He's not old. How old could he be? Fifty, fifty-five?

But he acts like he's old. He has no imagination. He's a bully. He doesn't know how to handle a woman. Maybe he never knew how to approach one.

He trembles. He breathes hard. He starts panting. His sweat drips onto my head. I'm trembling too. With disgust for myself.

Is it worth it, Adua, all this filth for a star, for a dressing room, for movies that mean nothing to you?

I wish I could ask Marilyn, but she's dead; she died badly, like so many, too many starlets with more tits than talent.

I wish I could ask Muna Kinky-Hair back in Somalia.

I know what she'd tell me: "Don't act like some saint, Adua," and, "you have to decide if you want to pay this price or not."

Did I want to or not? I couldn't tell. The price seemed too high and the product total junk.

I was confused.

I just know that Marilyn died badly. But at least Marilyn had a shred of talent. What about me? Do I?

Though talent certainly didn't save Marilyn. She died alone. She died badly. What about me? Will I?

Who will save me? I wonder. I want to shout the question. I don't have the courage. The magnate is already in position like a runner at the starting gate.

"Come here," he orders.

For the second time in one day I am on my knees in front of a man.

The first time was in the morning, in front of Nick. But that was a scene in the movie.

Fiction.

Nick … Nick Tonno, my partner, my costar, a homosexual, or as the director sometimes called him, "damned queer." I loved my crazy partner, that damned queer who the blessed heavens had led me to. Doing things with Nick is … was wonderful. He respects me. He guides me. He tells me: "This torture will be over soon, you and I deserve to shoot better movies."

I dream: "I want to be Judy Garland in *The Wizard of Oz*, singing and skipping around like a baby butterfly."

And he says: "What a vision you'd be in Dorothy's ruby slippers."

We position ourselves inside a car. We have to pretend we're making love. That's all I do in the movie, run naked on the beach and make love in the most absurd places. "Show more of the gap between your thighs," and with Nick's help I lift my skimpy slip higher. Nick rubs my head and reassures me: "It'll be over soon, hold on, think of Judy Garland."

Action, scene one, we're in a convertible. He kisses me. Nick is a good kisser. He's so tender. He doesn't want to eat me alive. "Do you want to get married?" I whisper to him. It seems like a line from our script, but it's actually from my heart. In that scene we don't need our voices. Arturo told us that the moans will be added in the dubbing studio. We just have to fake love talk and orgasm. I repeat the question: "Would you marry me, Nick?" And he replies:

"You know I can't, Adua, I'm a homosexual."

And I say:

"That's why I want to marry you. You wouldn't touch me like those other brutes, like Arturo does when he gets bored with his wife. You would respect me. I'd introduce you to my father and my aunt Fardosa."

"Are they nice?" Nick asks me. I don't know how to answer, just that I miss them. I feel like crying, but I don't want to ruin the scene. I cling to him desperately. He makes one of his killer faces and fake bites me on the neck like a vampire. It tickles and I start laughing, but to keep from ruining the scene I mime something that I have never experienced, that orgasm thing everyone's always talking about.

Nick always smells good.

Whereas the distributor, that bald magnate who I have to play nice with, the man who Sissi enigmatically calls the marquis, smells like garlic.

I go to open his fly. I want to get the whole thing over with quickly. "Just put it in my mouth and then it's good-bye, never see you again," I think. A flawless plan, I tell myself.

I open his fly. I avoid looking at that snake. It still repulses me. I don't look at it, I turn my eyes away. It scares me.

But I can't be scared right now. It's just a few seconds. I close my eyes. I grab it firm.

I take it in my mouth. It's done, I tell myself.

But the guy, this marquis, doesn't have an erection. His contraption dies in my mouth and a slimy rivulet drips pathetically onto the floor.

"Move, whore," he calls me.

The word doesn't offend me. That's what I am now. A whore, a sharmutta. That's what they've turned me into. In Somalia I was a young girl who was full of dreams and wanted to see the world. In just a few months they've manipulated, abused, used, transformed me. It feels like years, not months, have gone by. I feel so old, practically decrepit.

I wish I had some water. To get that sour taste out of my mouth. But the room is so dark. I can't see anything. Only the shadowy mahogany wood.

I see him crawl around the room like he's blind. Then he switches on the light. He puts himself together. I do too. We don't speak.

"You were good," he tells me. And he gives me a manly slap on the shoulder.

"Good?" I wonder silently. "We didn't do anything."

But I say nothing, it's better not to talk to that man. He's a bully, you can tell that he always wants to be right.

"Do you know how to dance?" he asks me.

"No," I reply curtly, irritated by such a personal question.

"Then you'll learn tonight. The other girls will teach you."

"Are we already going back out?"

"Yes, pet," he says, all sweet. I'm confused. I don't understand.

"Oh, and out there don't mention our little encounter, they wouldn't understand."

"I won't say a word, sir."

He likes being called sir.

"Tell Sissi that we'll distribute the movie well, we'll make you a little Negro star, you have nice legs, you deserve success."

We're almost at the door. I'm about to open it. He stops me. "Wait," he says.

"What?" I ask, a little dazed.

"I have a gift."

And he gives me a diamond gold bracelet. I don't know how to respond. "I'm a generous man, didn't Sissi tell you that?"

I say nothing. Better to keep quiet in certain circumstances.

I thank him. We return to the party.

His hand on my bottom. Like on the way there.

Back in the main room, he distributes big smiles. The other girls look at me and my bracelet with envy.

"Good, our little Adua," Sissi says to me, and fingering the bracelet she adds, "I see that you've done your duty."

I wanted to tell her the truth. But if I did that man would ruin me. He has the power to. He's filthy rich. He knows lots of people. Even in places where an honest person shouldn't be.

I keep quiet. I'm shaking. "I want to go."

"But now it's the best part, we're dancing."

"But I don't like to dance," I yell.

Everyone looks at me. A little stunned, clinking their glasses of champagne. "Don't yell, this is an elegant dinner," Sissi says.

And I don't yell. I bow my head. I cave.

Today I wouldn't bow my head. Today I would yell.

But today I'm old. Minutes, days, years have passed since that dinner. I've had a miscarriage, bad men, countless disappointments.

Today, though, I wouldn't bow my head. I wouldn't sell myself for a star on a dressing room door like that little girl I was.

The memory makes me yell.

Now I'm not quiet anymore. Yesterday, for example, I

yelled so loud that I scared my husband, my sweet little Titanic, nearly to death. In my sleep, I said: "No, it's not worth it to eat dirt for a star." And then I added: "You can't kill me without thinking I won't put up a fight." I started shaking violently.

And then my husband's big, strong, capable hands held me still.

"Adua, what's wrong? Adua, calm down! You're at home, with me. Adua …"

I looked at him with my eyes gaping. At first I didn't even recognize him. I was still lost in the haze of the distant past.

"Did you have a nightmare?" he asked me, concerned. How could I tell him the truth?

How could I tell him that unfortunately it wasn't a bad dream, just an unpleasant memory that comes to torment me every night? Later, I sold the bracelet. But the memory won't leave me alone. Every so often it comes and throws dismay in my face.

"Sorry," I whispered to my clueless husband.

"Sorry for what, Adua, you're delirious, you were yelling, did you know that? You screamed loud, you scared me. I'll go get you a glass of water."

"No, don't get me anything, just hold me."

And he did it even though, to tell the truth, he was a little annoyed.

26
TALKING-TO

It's so strange not having you around anymore, Adua.

Why did you leave? After all, I never treated you badly. You had a roof over your head, and food too. I always gave you the first fruit ... remember that sweet papaya that day? From Afgooye. You liked it so much. You smiled at me. And I smiled at you too. In my way, I smiled at you. Sure, my mustache hides my mouth, but I can smile like everybody else. All of you always described me as a grouch. When you were under my roof you had meat on your bones, you were pretty, solid, like a woman should be. And I raised you. I raised you well. There's not a girl raised better in this whole dirty country. I worked as hard as I could to make you into a woman of fortitude. I couldn't bear the idea of you becoming like your mother. Your mother was a zombie. Inept, starry-eyed, sluggish. She was slow, your mother. Extremely slow. I was the only thought she had.

Her brain, besides me, contained nothing.

27

ZOPPE

Zoppe loathed Mogadishu. He couldn't stand its slightly sweet odor. Mogadishu made his stomach turn, with its well-to-do air and white buildings. In Mogadishu he felt like a foreigner. Someone from down south, a yokel from Magalo, whom the residents looked at snobbishly and even with a certain pity. When he was little, his father often dragged him to that city "to which we owe so much, my son." Zoppe would come up with a million excuses not to go. Once it was an upset stomach, another time a high fever. He didn't want to set foot in the capital. And he didn't care that he owed his life to it, he truly didn't. But Haji Safar, who knew how to read his boy's heart, tugged him affectionately, saying: "Come on, lazy. That won't work with me. Get your bag ready, we're going." And that's how the boy bowed his head and obeyed his father every time.

But everything was different that day. Haji Safar wasn't by his side. Zoppe had come with the Italians. Returned as a servant. A tool in rapacious hands.

During the trip from Massawa to Mogadishu, Zoppe couldn't manage to think of anything else besides his misfortune.

On the ship, he wrestled with the dark visions that appeared to him so vividly.

Detached rooster heads, tongues hanging from pomegranate trees, a sea red with blood, and him with wounds all over his back. And as the voyage slowly progressed and he could feel Mogadishu approaching, his visions became even more outrageous. A man riding a leopard laughed wildly, while a crow made a nest on the snakelike head of a monster with swollen lips. Zoppe didn't recognize anything. In those monstrous visions nothing had a human form. People with three layers of teeth were talking to oxen that had rabbit ears, and crouched down next to them was a creature with a giraffe's head excreting butterflies over a pile of corpses. Massawa …

Damned city! The memory of it was driving him mad.

"Mister, mister … are you all right?"

It was Uarda, one of the serving girls from the farmhouse where they were staying, who jolted him back to the present.

"Yes, fine," replied Zoppe. "The air of Mogadishu is dizzying."

"You were talking to yourself, did you know that?" the girl laughed.

Zoppe was annoyed by the impertinent observation, but he didn't reply lest he feel even dumber. He examined her. Uarda was pretty, very pretty. Tall, perky breasts, heart-shaped derriere.

"I have a headache," Zoppe said.

He wanted to say more to her. Like: "Run, get far away from here." Instead he just looked at her. Maybe she was an orphan. Otherwise no one would have sent her to serve an Italian. Everyone in Mogadishu knew what happened to Uardas in Italian houses.

Zoppe suddenly felt drained. Weak. "Damn count," he muttered to himself.

It was a nice house, the one that the Italian governorate in Mogadishu had provided Celestino Anselmi. A typical colonial structure with a Moorish staircase leading to the upper floors. The stark white building fell into a certain harmony with the lush tropical garden surrounding it. "I'm going to have a big party here tonight. I deserve it."

Zoppe only replied, "Yes, sir."

"The senses dance in this city, my dear boy."

Zoppe looked up at the sky. There wouldn't be any party. The southwest monsoon, the one that made even the jinns tremble, was coming. "Soon it'll beat down on the city and the damned count's head," Zoppe thought. And that consoled him.

•

He and his father didn't have an appointment with a date, time or place. There was no "See you then," between them. Father and son could meet just by thinking of each other.

And Fakr ad-Din was the only place where his father would have met him in Mogadishu. It was their treasured place in that foreign-seeming city.

As a little boy, Zoppe spent hours contemplating the verses from the sura of The Cow from the Koran magisterially carved in Kufic script over the door. It was pure joy for him to just stand there at the threshold where the light chased the shadow between the thin marble columns.

"There was a time," Haji Safar had told him, "the time of our ancestors, when this mosque was as big as the portion of sky contained in the eyes of an angel."

In that mosque, repentant jinns asked forgiveness to heaven before taking their last breath, and souls brimming with love for creation sought refuge from the evils of the world.

"If for some reason I don't die in our holy city," Haji Safar said, "you, my adored son, will take me, emaciated and near death, on your shoulders, and bring me here." At Fakr ad-Din anything was possible. Zoppe had experienced it for himself.

It was there that he had seen a pink man for the first time. Zoppe was small for his age and much bonier. In fact the women insisted that Haji Safar have him eat chicken broth and dates to keep him alive.

"Doesn't this child have a mother?"

"She died bringing him into the world. But he has my wives to take care of him. Fawzia, Alia, Halima coddle him as if he were their child, fruit of their own womb. He couldn't be in better hands."

"But why do these sticks hold him up, like an old paralytic?"

It was in those moments when Haji Safar deplored human souls. Men of dust who condemned their neighbor's every flaw.

And he, Haji, didn't want to yield to that brutality. Of course his son had suffered, a high rheumatic fever had struck him in his sleep a year earlier and nearly killed him. But it wasn't his time and he was spared. That's all that counted. Ultimately, just that.

"You will overcome, my son," he said. "You won't notice the difference between you and your peers. And I swear to you on my name and my honor that soon I'll see you run like an ostrich through the endless savannah."

Zoppe looked at his father with trust. He really hoped he would be able to run and play like the other kids.

Then one night, one of those agitated by dreams and chimeras, an image was imprinted on Haji's mind. "That," the old wise man said with surprise, "is the door to the Fakr ad-Din mosque. So Mogadishu is the place where I must take my son, that's where I will finally see him run." And the next day he prepared for the journey.

He spent two nights and two days mixing the ointments he would rub onto his son's battered legs.

"This herb, husband, is called devil's claw, but really it's made from the nails of angels. If the little one's muscles are inflamed it will dull the pain," said Fawzia, the first of his wives.

"And this one is blackcurrant," said his second wife, Halima. "My brother, the merchant, brought it for me as a gift. It is from the rocky mountains of Asia. Its bark is smooth. If fear comes to torment little Zoppe's leg, this plant will know what to do."

"Here, dear, in my hands is prickly little aloe," said Alia with a laugh, his last wife. "It will bring you good dreams and helps with digestion."

Haji Safar thanked his three wives for such sweet gifts. He said "thank you" because those were the only right words to say.

After the morning prayer, father and son set off for Mogadishu, heading away from their beautiful blue sea.

They immediately entered the barren bush. No living thing crossed their path the first day. Only a vulture followed them overhead in hopes of seeing them take a wrong step. But Haji Safar had traveled those paths for years. He knew the secrets of the seemingly hostile land. Zoppe, to entertain himself, watched the ants, intent on their endless work. Diligent, they hauled bits of meat on their little backs, perhaps left over from some hyena's meal. The first night, restless owls made the little one nervous. "They're trills of love," Haji Safar explained, and Zoppe, who had no interest in that explanation, said: "Father, when will we see the sea again?"

The second day they came upon some shepherds. They slept with them in empty *tukuls* and satisfied their thirst with the goat milk they were offered. They also spent their third day with the shepherds. On the fourth, Haji Safar said: "We must leave you. We have to cross the sea."

Their donkey was tired. Haji Safar petted his neck affectionately. "Not much longer, my old man. Just one more little push and we will reach the place we need to reach."

It was after these words that the dry smell of the bush was replaced by the sudden scent of cinnamon.

"Smell that, son?" Haji Safar asked, excited. "That's the smell of Mogadishu."

Zoppe was overwhelmed by that chaos of sounds and smells so different from one another.

Then he saw the colors. He saw the yellow of smiles, the purple of violence, the green of resignation, the pink of tears. The people in Mogadishu wailed. They wailed like an African wild dog about to die. They wailed over unsettled accounts, love gone wrong, a pound of meat that wasn't enough to feed a family. Haji Safar and Zoppe went through a covered market and the boy was fascinated by the mechanical precision of the goldsmiths at work.

A flash of greed appeared in the little one's eyes. He wanted to stay there forever, cover himself in that marvelous gold.

But the donkey didn't stop. This wasn't their destination. They walked for another hour. Then they saw in the middle of an ochre expanse a crane regal in its posture.

"It's a sign," said Haji Safar, who stopped the donkey and his step. "This is where what is to happen will happen."

The mosque was in sight, but still far away.

"I'll be right back. Wait for me here," Haji Safar told his son. And he left him alone.

And that was when, all of a sudden, the pink man appeared.

On his face was a long yellow beard and on his head a few fog-colored curls. He was dressed in a long black cloth, his feet weren't visible, his hands just barely, and they were pink too.

"What if he eats me?" Zoppe thought.

"Father," he started shouting, "Father, where are you?" "I'm here, can you see me? In front of this big door."

Zoppe wondered how to reach him. And that was how he began slowly crawling up the mound leading to the mosque entrance, dragging his crutches behind him.

The pink man, at the sight of the crawling boy, thought in his mercy to help him. *"Aniga waxaan ahay saaxiibka."* I am your friend. Those poorly pronounced words were for little Zoppe the beginning of the end.

He tossed his crutches aside and began running like mad. Running toward his father, toward salvation.

"A miracle!" cried Haji Safar.

And he too ran barefoot toward his son. He lifted the boy, hugged him close, became a father again, and covered him in kisses.

The word "miracle" provoked a delirium. Word spread inside the mosque and even the imam, with a trail of believers in tow, wanted to come and see. Excitement overwhelmed the old soothsayer like nothing ever before.

And he began saying how merciful Allah had been charitable with him and his little Zoppe. "Now if he wants, he'll be able to fly with the falcons at sunset."

As he waited for his father to appear, Zoppe thought of this bond between them that had never faltered. "I'm sure I'll see him here. It's our soul place."

.

"Father, don't leave me," he murmured, his lips dry from all the excitement.

Bitter tears lined his well-fed face and he tried to wipe them away quickly with the sleeves of his jelabiyad.

Over his head a falcon spotted some lost chicks, while a cat looked for a secluded cave to take his final breath in solitude.

Then the baboon appeared.

He looked at Zoppe through his spotted mask and seemed to laugh at his desperation. Zoppe wanted nothing more than to throw a rock at that cheeky baboon.

But something, or someone, stayed his hand.

The baboon sat on his two feet, his head turned eastward to greet the sun. He raised his free hands, revealing a moon-shaped object clutched in his right hand and displayed like a trophy.

Then without warning the baboon jumped on him. Aiming right for the turban. "What are you doing, you stupid animal?" he yelled.

Something had gotten into that baboon and he had no

intention of releasing his prey. Zoppe gave up on getting it back.

"Ah, what a nice breeze," he remarked. He was grateful to his outburst for liberating him from that servitude.

"How did you know I hate that turban?"

The baboon indicated the sun, shaking his hands frantically.

"You're a strange beast, you are." Zoppe chuckled, toying with the dry twigs around him.

These had been frenetic and painful days for him.

"Ah, baboon, if only you could give my tormented soul a little relief."

The baboon started dancing. He showed off his red bottom irreverently and Zoppe laughed heartily.

"You monkeys are unpredictable."

The baboon shook his head and made a loud noise.

"What do you know about it, huh? You shake your head like that just for fun. You have no idea what I saw last night. I was awake, not dreaming. If you had seen what I saw you'd quit your laughing and would be crying with me."

And Zoppe began to spew words and images. "Last night I saw nothing but death around me. I saw mangled black bodies. Hanged men, houses burned down, hands cut off, decapitated heads stuck on spears, stabbed women, disfigured corpses, children tied up and dragged while still alive, deacons executed, little girls raped. I saw blood, pus, brains. And I saw heads severed from their bodies placed on silver trays surrounded by people laughing. The heads belonged to Ethiopians and the smiling mouths to Italians. I saw them making fun of the corpses and taking pictures of them. Then I saw them wrapping the photos of the horrors to send as gifts to their girlfriends in Italy."

Zoppe put his face in his hands and cried like a little child.

"I sold myself like the Christian Judas for a pile of money. If those people die it's also my fault. How will I be able to look my friend Dagmawi in the eyes? It would have been better if I'd never been born and my father's seed had dried up."

Zoppe doubled over like a wounded zebra.

The baboon came near him and started purring like a cat.

"You're sweet, baboon. But you can't understand me. No one can understand me. I can see things before other men, but I wasn't granted the power to change the future, neither theirs nor mine."

The baboon shook his head.

"But … but … so you do understand?"

Zoppe looked at the half-moon that the animal was holding in his hands. That was when he realized. The baboon was none other than his father, Haji Safar. The old man had kept their appointment.

28
ADUA

Lul told me that Labo Dhegax, my house in Magalo, is worth its weight in gold. "I had it appraised for you, honey."

"Well then?" I asked with a lump in my throat that made me greedier than I actually am.

"Well, the profit would be about a million dollars, give or take a few cents, a net profit, to be clear."

I said: "Net, sister?"

"Yes, dear, you would pocket a cool million dirty American dollars, aren't you happy?"

I sank down to the floor. I'd half-fainted, as if someone had given me horrible news. I tried to take deep breaths. I tried to revive the beats in my time-ravaged heart.

"A million dollars?" I repeated like an idiot. It was a number out of an American TV show, a mafia deal, money laundering, not something I could grasp in my little, old lady reality.

"But are all the prices for houses and land in Somalia that high?" I asked, stunned.

"The real estate bubble has peaked and houses are worth gold, sister. And you know, there's oil here. Everyone is selling, buying, quoting, appraising. It's like the Wall Street stock exchange. Sure, in Mogadishu everything is more expensive, more inflated, but even in Magalo, I promise you, you can make some big figure deals."

"A million dollars? Is that possible? For my rickety old house?"

"The time to make deals won't last forever, my sister. We have to go for it now, before it's too late. Now that they've caught a whiff of oil, it's easy money, but soon they'll realize that Somalia is a rip-off and the bubble will burst in the sun. And the houses will go back to being the trash they always were."

I liked it when Lul made herself my own personal guardian spirit. It was comforting to know that she was always by my side thinking about my needs.

Meanwhile, that exorbitant figure whirled around in my head: a million dollars. I'd never seen that much money in my life.

In general money and I have never gotten along. I've always spent it badly and in the brief period when I did have some I let myself get hustled like a fool.

"Get on a plane and come down here. Happiness is here," my Lul told me. An electronic voice broke into our excited conversation and cut off the line.

"Lul," I yelled. Lul …

Ah, I really could have used a Lul in 1977. Of course I hadn't been offered a million dollars then, but a decent stack of Italian lire, yes. And there were the American studios, that small part in a Bond movie they wanted to offer me and that I was dying to play.

But …

But in 1977 there was no Lul to help me. I was alone as a dog and completely at the mercy of Sissi and Arturo. That's why everything went wrong after a while.

If she had been by my side, I wouldn't have ended up penniless, drained dry and duped like a dunce by those lowlifes. Lul would have told me: "You need an agent, honey," and "make sure to read every clause in the contract you sign." If Lul had been there I wouldn't have frozen to death in a miserable little room in a pension on Via Cavour. She would have demanded a bathtub, room service, soft pillows, a dignified wardrobe, comfortable shoes, clean and ironed sheets.

She would have slapped Sissi and called her a user. And Sissi wouldn't have dared say to me: "What extravagant requests you have, Adua," or "What a spoiled Negro you are." Lul certainly wouldn't have sent me around in unseemly little rags and with all my skin hanging out. If Lul had been there, Arturo wouldn't have touched me nor would the marquis have laid his hands on my backside. Lul would have kept me away from the drugs, alcohol, cheap cigarettes, fried food, men who wanted only my body.

Lul would have brought me back to our traditions. And she would have put me on a diet and would have allowed me sweets only as a treat on Sunday mornings.

If Lul had been there I wouldn't have spent so much time crying alone. She would have taken me on walks down Via del Corso to get gelato at Giolitti. If Lul had been there she would have called me at least twice a day, even just to tell me: "I'm so glad you exist in the world." And then Lul would have told me loud and clear to forget about Nick Tonno. "He's homosexual, he can't love you. Get it in your head, abaayo." Of course she would have advised me to stop obsessing over him, standing below his house every night, buying him flowers I couldn't afford. "He can only give you friendship, nothing more, accept it and move on."

If Lul had been there she would have made me finish school. She would have pulled me by the ear and shoved my nose in the pages of a dictionary. "Without languages you're nobody," she would have told me, and after a certain weighty pause she'd have added, "but without your own you're lost." If Lul had been there they wouldn't have made me sign one-sided contracts where I ceded all interest in my name and all merchandising of my character. If Lul had been there I wouldn't have lost millions of old lire by forgetting to register my official residency at the police station, and with the Italian social security administration. If Lul had been there I would have had proper documents from the very beginning and the opportunity to become an Italian citizen after five years. If Lul had been there I wouldn't have exhibited myself at seedy promotional events where drunk men slipped bills in my

green garter, barking unspeakable obscenities at me. Lul
would have demanded respect for my person and I think
she would have also intervened with the movie script. She
wouldn't have let me do all those nude running scenes
and she would have objected to shooting on the beach
in the cold. She would have said something like: "If you
want her to run as God made her then rent a set in the
Caribbean and not in Capocotta." If Lul had been there
she would have checked the press every day to see what
came out about the movie and about me. She would have
spared me the pain of headlines like "Burning Hot Black
Hole" or "Steamy Kiss from the Abyssinian Abyss." She
would have demanded a title for me that was certainly
more dignified than "black Venus" and she would have
been furious if anyone said to me on the street, "Hey,
black beauty, I'd ride you right now." If Lul had been
there she would have dragged me to the piazza with the
women who were protesting for the right to an abor-
tion and she would have shown me that those women
were also fighting for my rights, to free my body from
the drool-covered desires of a decadent society. If Lul
had been there she would have stopped me from depil-
ating myself like a white woman: "But if Somalis aren't
hairy, what are you removing?" And Lul would have also
forbidden me to use whitening creams, saying: "Are you
crazy? They cause skin cancer! And you fool, your skin
tone is beautiful!" And then Lul, I'm sure of it, would
have objected like a maniac to my straightening my hair.

"You're ridiculous with this spaghetti, it's not believable, Adua," and she would have made me feel how much better it was to be free and keep your own curly hair. And if Lul had been there she would have taught me to be proud of myself. She would have recited my family tree like a poem in hendecasyllables and then she would have said: "You were born from these ancestors' bones, don't forget their bones, your roots." If Lul had been there she would have forced me to call my father. "Parents must be loved." And she would have whispered in my ear: "Because you don't know when God will call them back to Him." If Lul had been there I wouldn't have made that movie with Arturo, that ugly, obscene movie.

29

TALKING-TO

I saw you. There you were, dressed like an old woman, surrounded by beggars. I saw you, Adua. You didn't have the courage to enter, to look me in the face, to confront me. Do I really scare you that much, my daughter?

I saw your movie. I cried.

I don't cry. But watching your movie, I cried. I have failed in this life. If I let my own humiliation come to you it only means that I have failed. I don't know how to treat others, Adua. I didn't know how to treat that fool, your mother. She loved me too much, the fool. They called her Asha the Rash because deep down she was reckless and she liked to take on lost causes. I was the biggest lost cause of all. She fell in love with my needy eyes. And I, instead of taking her love, went against it. I tried to destroy her and her love along with her. No one has ever loved me so much in this life. No one has ever proven me so right and so wrong. Asha, your mother, wanted to guide me. She'd tell me: "What do you expect from the past? Now you can make up for it. Now you can fix everything. You can be better." She was always enthusiastic, always optimistic. She died with her optimism. When she brought you into the world, she lasted long enough to see you. She lay her eyes on you and then she expired with a smile. When I saw that life was going out of her I yelled like a madman, I nearly dropped you. The women, diligent, ran over to grab you from my fragile hands. And from that moment on I couldn't be alone with you. Between us I put indifference, then an invented hate, a terror remote-controlled like those toy cars kids play with today. I don't know, I didn't know how to be a father. Maybe I owe you an apology. But I can't. I don't know how to use certain words. But I can tell you one thing: watching that movie, I realized how much you've suffered in this life. In the end, you and I are no different, someone humiliated us, put us down. I stayed down. Maybe things will turn out better for you. Maybe.

30

ZOPPE

"Sheeko sheeko, sheeko xariir."

Story story, story of silk.

That's how all the tales Zoppe heard as a boy began. After the evening prayer, his father would call him over, and he would curl up sweetly at his feet. It was the only place where he felt truly safe. The only place where he felt alive. His father had a strong and sincere voice. A voice that opened up to all magic. The words flowed one after another and created worlds where even a baby chick could rise to the occasion and become the bravest of warriors. Haji Safar knew how to make him laugh, but then without warning he would plunge his son into inaccessible lows. All those demons filling the scenes scared little Zoppe to death. But there was always a clever shepherdess to cheer him up. Howa, Araweelo, Wil Wal—he quickly learned the names of the extraordinary characters that populated his father's tales. Then one day he grew too big to curl up at his father's feet, and just as it had begun, that flow of stories stopped. But the words didn't. They underwent a change. Zoppe was a man now and Haji Safar relied on him for household matters. Every so often politics would come up in conversation too. But it was the stories of their ancestors that bound the old father to his beloved son. Ancient stories scented with cinnamon and cardamom. It was always the father who would speak. Zoppe would just nod or cock his head in a sign of contentment. He didn't want to destroy those moments with his sharp voice and sputtering rage. He preferred to keep quiet. But that day, at the clearing in front of the Fakr ad-Din mosque, the roles were reversed. It was the father who wanted to hear the son's story. It was Haji Safar who strained his ears to catch every sound that came out of Zoppe's mouth.

"Massawa … that's the city I got lost in, Father." Massawa …

It had happened a few days before. Zoppe couldn't manage to get that cursed place out of his head. It was a port, an inlet, one of the most important cities in Eritrea, that country the Italians insisted on calling the founding colony and which the most inveterate fascists considered the outpost of the empire. The count had an appointment that morning and judging by his pace, he didn't want to be late. They quickly crossed through the market. And Zoppe's spirit, despite the rush, was captivated by the showy spectacle that East Africa offered. Languages mixed together in a magical alchemy fused by the sharp taste of dates from Egias. The girls flapped their fans to drive away the voracious flies trying to dirty the blocks of tamarind. The melons from inland and the watermelons grown along the border stood out at the richer stands.

Sweet potatoes were everywhere, even on the ground, with the risk of tripping. But what made Zoppe's heart burst were the little fish fried in big vats of oil. The fish were immersed for a few seconds, just enough time to quiver, and then they were eaten hot with pita baked in terracotta pots. If he had been alone he would have made a buffet of those little fried fish. But Count Anselmi's steps were too fast and they tore him away. The count moved like a hyena that has spotted its prey. He darted confidently through the labyrinth of narrow streets in the port district.

Massawa was a city he knew well. They shot through the dark. That shadowy race foresaw no stops.

"Will it be much longer, Count?"

No answer. Just a grunt. And Zoppe realized he was in trouble.

·

Damp and darkness. Zoppe was greeted by the familiar scent of rats. He felt trapped without understanding why. His eyes slowly adjusted to the darkness. He sensed that the room was small and very crowded. Shadows popped out from everywhere, and little by little took shape.

"Zoppe, listen well, translate every word, don't leave out even a sigh." The count was clear. Not even a sigh.

In the middle of that darkness were two men surrounded by servants. A wrinkled old man with eyes like an octopus and a curly-haired young man with fine lips. The old man was sitting on a cart. He was wearing a white tunic embroidered with gold. A servant, Zoppe noted with dismay, shaded his master under a little white parasol. Zoppe wondered from what. The servant was breathing hard and Zoppe was worried.

They were Ethiopian dignitaries, he could tell by their expensive and ornate dress.

What were they doing in Massawa, in enemy territory?

His attention shifted to the young man with delicate lips, the old man's grandson or late-born son. His hair was a messy pile of curls and mist that he struggled to keep under control. He smelled like coconut and jasmine. His chin was receding and his dark eyes deep set. His aquiline nose towered imperiously over a gaunt face that had little royalty in it. Nothing about that young man seemed solid. That was clear from the demeanor of his servants, who paid him little attention. He was wearing a suit, a souvenir from the West, fit to bursting, the sleeves too short for his long arms. And the tails dangled flaccidly over his chicken legs. Zoppe found the situation very odd. But he didn't say a word about it.

He didn't ask questions. He just got ready to translate. He had to do his job well, it was the only way he could earn his freedom. And perhaps—why not—a little cash. He had to be prompt and precise. Translate word by word. He couldn't judge. Open and close his mouth, that was his task. Nothing more. He couldn't think. He couldn't interfere. He couldn't improve. He had to just open and close his mouth.

He looked at the old man sitting on the cart. There was something disturbing about his posture. His spine was curved in on itself and it made him into a pile of rags. But it was his hands, which the old man kept in plain sight, that worried him. They were nervous hands, shaking, with pale nails. Hands that looked a little like the claws of a bird of prey. Demanding, ferocious hands. Hands that were perhaps stained with innocent blood. Where did those hands come from? From what part of Ethiopia? Zoppe asked himself if he would be able to translate all the cruelty contained in those hands.

Especially in those fat fingers. They seemed on the verge of exploding. "What if I can't do it? What if I don't understand? Who knows what dialect of Amharic this guy speaks." He started to tremble. Beads of sweat gathered on his forehead. He who knew all the languages of East Africa now was afraid of being left speechless. A rank terror seized him by the gut. It was as if a vortex had suddenly appeared in his head. And everything he knew had been swallowed by it. For a moment Zoppe couldn't even remember his own name.

•

Zoppe's head started spinning. There was something different about that day, that smell, those faces, that room. He looked at the old man and his son. And then his eyes moved to the servants. They all had the same expression, same nose, same absent air. They were tired, fed up, mad or maybe just resigned. They all had curly hair and amber skin, a jangling belt and big ears. Together they formed a flat expanse of black skin and stifled sentiments. There was something familiar and perverse in that picture. But Zoppe couldn't seem to figure out what. Then almost unexpectedly came the old man's first words, jolting him from his venomous thoughts.

"*Tena yistilign,*" he began.

Zoppe had to focus on that opaque, translucent voice. It was beautiful. A rugged singsong that could awaken a sleep-soothed soul to new life. But his words were harsh, sharp, horrible. Zoppe couldn't stop to think about their meaning, because then he wouldn't have translated anything. He would have been lost. A carcass that even a vulture would have left alone. The old man's eyes dominated the dark. They stood out imperiously in that room that smelled of rats. But it was Count Anselmi's cannibal gaze that confused Zoppe. His aristocratic grace was gone. The count's Italian, once pleasant, had become a primordial scream. Even his once-elegant hands were the hoofs of a warthog in heat. In the middle of these people Zoppe felt alone. Traversed by the poisoned arrows of betrayal. Every word wounded him. Every gesture outraged him. The old man was offering Italy his support for the upcoming war. He would supply arms, men, refreshment, provisions. He promised to kill Emperor Haile Selassie himself, if necessary. The old man was signing a blood pact with Italy, from which there was no return. And he, Zoppe, was translating it. No, he couldn't think about it. He had to open and close his mouth. That's all. Open and close his mouth. Leave nothing out. Not even the sighs.

The count gladly accepted and promised the pathetic old man a grand career for his son. "You won't have anything to fear with us." And with that, he tossed a wad of Ethiopian talleros in the air, which the old man awkwardly tried to grab. "Naturally, you'll be compensated for your loyalty to Italy." Another rainfall of talleros went through the room. The count laughed with satisfaction. It had been so easy to buy off those Negroes. Child's play leading them to betray their own people. At that moment the old man yelled over to his son: "Thank the gentle count who has been so good to us." The young man, who hadn't moved a muscle throughout that entire discussion, began to awaken like a big golem dulled by time. In an instant he had thrown himself at the count's feet and was kissing the muddy toes of his boots.

EPILOGUE:
PIAZZA DEI CINQUECENTO

Je demande qu'on me considère à partir de mon Désir.
As soon as I desire I am asking to be considered.
—Frantz Fanon

He left. Two hours ago now.

I put him on a high-speed train for Milan. He'll figure it out from there. He has the other tickets. The fat man helping us said he would take care of everything. That he has ferried hundreds of people all over Europe. And that with him there was no risk of being caught by the border police. "It's a cinch," he said. And he added: "But you need nice clothes, recognizable brands, maybe a nice jacket— he has to look respectable." So a couple of hours before- hand, we went to a store downtown and bought two pairs of pants, the kind businessmen wear to pick up girls on the weekends, two dress shirts, the usual white one and blue one, and some decent shoes. Dressed up like that my little Titanic looked like a man about town. He was handsome in those clothes that were so removed from his life experience.

"Have an intelligent look on your face during the trip," the smuggler told him. "They can't see a starving refugee, a dirty Somali, a nervous wreck. You have to radiate confidence from every pore. Make the world believe you're in control and don't have a care in the world." The fat smuggler, who was named Omar like all the rest of them, advised my little Titanic to get into character. "You should seem like a student or a guy on a weekend getaway. Be cool, basically." All the way through Ventimiglia the trip would be smooth, and after that it would be in the hands of God and the smugglers. I paid dearly for that trip. It cost me a lot. I couldn't have imagined how much those trips cost.

Bastards!

"You shouldn't complain," Omar told me with a smirk. "My prices are competitive and with me you can be sure that your little friend will reach his destination safe and sound."

"But, lady," he warned, "you have to forget about Sweden. At most, he can shoot for Germany. At least if they take his fingerprints there, there's a good chance they'll keep him and won't return him to sender. Just say you were mistreated in Italy and they'll let you stay in Germany. The Germans care about human rights; after the Holocaust they have to be nice."

Omar made me sick.

"Let's go for Germany," my husband said. "As long as you get me away from here." I wanted him to get away too.

"I won't come with you to the train," I said as we crossed Piazza dei Cinquecento. "From here on you'll have to manage alone. And I've never liked good-byes."

I looked around. The piazza was pandemonium, enveloped in the exhaust of the buses occupying every space in the terminus like beached whales. People zigzagged frenetically and even the most elderly were possessed by a delirious hunger for speed. They ran obliquely toward an uncertain, often completely chance future. Piazza dei Cinquecento seemed more like a freeway than a piazza. It wasn't a place to stop and chat. The words would get lost in an incoherent, sometimes disturbing rumble. Piazza dei Cinquecento was wrapped up with my history like nowhere else. Piazza of migrants, first arrivals, departures, my many regrets. In that piazza, so disconnected from itself, I had found and lost myself a thousand times. I remember when, in those early, crazy years, posing as an actress, I crossed it half-naked in skimpy clothes, because Sissi, always Sissi, had ordered me to show off my beauty to Rome. And I obeyed. This is where I came to know infamy. But it is also here that, thanks to my friend Lul, years later, I made myself a new life. More serious, modest, sensible clothes. Here, in the darkest years, I rediscovered the smile of my people. Behind the station, they sold the *xalwo* I was crazy about. I had to cross Piazza dei Cinquecento to get to that strange Somalia that had developed in the back streets of the station neighborhood. I even met my Titanic in Piazza dei Cinquecento. Drunk, he'd hang around different areas of Rome: Corso Italia, Piazza Vittorio, Ponte Lungo. But it was in Piazza dei Cinquecento that I saw him bellowing profanities with malicious gin flowing through his veins. It is there, in that piazza that Italy had dedicated to its fallen soldiers in East Africa, that I'd manufactured a papier-mâché love.

Suddenly I saw something loom over my head. Something white and shiny. "Get down, duck," my husband yelled.

But I was blinded by the whiteness, I couldn't move. It was the most beautiful thing I'd ever seen in my life.

Then I noticed something yellow. All wrinkled. I don't know when I realized that it was the yellow of a bird's feet. It flew over me. And without my catching a good look, it took my turban. Tore it off violently.

"Cover your face or it'll scratch you, Adua."

I couldn't understand why that seagull had targeted me.

"They're going to eat us," a man said, "like in that Hitchcock movie." A woman asked if I needed help.

I yelled to my husband: "See that bird, just sitting there looking at us, do you see how it's looking at us?"

And it was true. It was staring at me.

"Take the cloth, save the cloth," I said to my Titanic. But my husband didn't move.

The seagull stared at me again. It was as if it wanted to tell me something. Apologize.

Then it started pecking at the fabric. "Stop it," I yelled to my Titanic. But my husband didn't move.

The seagull made a disaster of the fabric with its pointy beak. "Stop it, please," I begged.

"No, Adua," he replied. "I won't, that seagull did us a favor. If only I'd had the guts."

"How dare you!"

"You looked terrible with that dull rag on your head. Right over there, at Habshiro, they sell scarves from the Emirates, the latest fashion. Now my wife will be beautiful and chic too. A veil in red, in green, one for all the days of the week."

It was my father's, that turban.

I had snatched it one afternoon in Somalia, ages ago.

The very day I had gone to Magalo for the premiere of my movie. A premiere that never happened. My father paid the manager of Cinema Munar the equivalent of three full houses for them not to show it.

Three showings ... Was that my price tag?

Three showings was what I was worth to my father, three showings.

Three showings for him not to look bad, not to disgrace the family name, so he could keep on pretending to have a daughter.

My price.

Three showings not to see me, to erase me, not to be ashamed. My father had broken my heart once again.

That day, step by step, my feet took me to what had once been my house.

I wanted to be Marilyn, I wanted to be Audrey, I wanted to be Katharine or at least Kim Novak.

I wanted to tap dance like Ginger Rogers and do the splits like Cyd Charisse.

I wanted flowers from Gene Kelly and looks full of respect from a passing Jimmy Stewart.

I wanted the white clothes, the crinolines, the puffy sleeves.

I wanted Billy Wilder to make me an icon and Errol Flynn to come and save me.

But most of all I'd have liked to be Ruby Dee. Ruby was black like me. And she didn't have to sell herself. Ruby fought for civil rights. I never fought for anything.

I was swathed in leopard skins and I ran as naked as Eve the sinner. I was always chased by a serpent.

Always hounded by shame. I was tired, so tired.

That was when, almost by accident, my eye fell on the clothes hung out to dry. A listless look, devoid of nerve.

But it was enough to fill my field of vision with sheets, tops, wraps, *garees* and *guntiino*. The blue stuck out in all that white.

I would have recognized that blue out of a thousand blues. I knew that cloth well. My father wrapped it around his head and never took it off.

"So he does take it off every once in a while," I said to myself. In a flash I went and stole the cloth.

I didn't see my father that day.

I didn't see my father any other day.

I never saw him again, to tell the truth.

All I had left of him was that blue strip of cloth, that strange turban, which up until a few hours ago I wouldn't have taken off for anything in the world.

And then that seagull, with one swoop, in the middle of Piazza dei Cinquecento, ripped it away from me.

Do you realize, my little elephant, what it had done?

It was the sign of my slavery and my old shame, that turban. It was the yoke I had chosen to redeem myself.

What would I do now without my slavery on my head? How would I atone for everything I'd done now?

"Ahmed," I finally asked, calling my husband by name, "why didn't you help me?"

"I did help you," Ahmed said, with an amused look. "That bird was sent by heaven."

"Really?"

"Really."

Ahmed … ah, Ahmed, I'm going to miss you.

I had never realized up until that moment how much that boy I picked up at the station loved me. I've been horrible for calling him Titanic all this time.

Oh, little elephant, how many mistakes I make. I miss my father and my husband.

Ahmed even gave me a gift, just imagine.

"I got this for you," he said. "I didn't want to leave without giving you a gift." It was a big package.

I tore off the yellow wrapping paper.

It was incredible to see that my husband—he still was my husband—had bought me a video camera.

"Where did you find this kind of money?"

"I borrowed some, nothing big, and some friends helped me out."

"Really?"

"I never gave you gifts. And I was sorry to leave without a little something for you.

You've been kind. You saved me. You loved me. I'm grateful to you for that."

"Thanks," I whispered.

Ahmed took me in his arms, in the middle of that Capitoline chaos.

And then he said, "Now you can film whatever you want, now you can tell your story however you think and you feel."

"Seriously?"

"Yes, seriously. And finally you'll be able to discover what there is across the sea." Around us, Piazza dei Cinquecento was smiling.

HISTORICAL NOTE

This novel weaves together three historical moments: Italian colonialism, 1970s Somalia, and our present day, which has seen the Mediterranean transformed into an open grave of migrants.

The characters in *Adua* balance on the architecture of this multivoiced story and in a certain sense make it their own. Over the course of the narrative I have not analyzed these periods in detail because I wanted to transform historical events into emotions, visions, experiences.

But now I'd like to provide a little more information about the context and background of my characters.

Italian colonialism has been one of the great repressions of the country's historiography. Only thanks to Angelo Del Boca's monumental work *Gli Italiani in Africa Orientale* (The Italians in East Africa, Laterza 1976, now reprinted by Mondadori) was a topic long swept under a rug of silence finally addressed. Fortunately, today we have a vast choice of historical and other texts. In particular, I recommend: Nicola Labanca, *Oltremare. Storia dell'espansione coloniale italiana* (Overseas: A History of Italian Colonial Expansion, Il Mulino, 2002); Giulietta

Stefani, *Colonia per maschi* (A Colony for Men, Ombre Corte Editore, 2007); David Forgacs, *Italy's Margins: Social Exclusion and Nation Formation since 1861* (Cambridge University Press, 2014); Ruth Ben-Ghiat, *Italian Fascism's Empire Cinema* (Indiana University Press, 2015) and Ennio Flaiano's novel *Tempo di Uccidere* (*A Time to Kill*, Quartet Books, 1992).

It is often erroneously believed that colonialism was merely the work of fascism, when instead it characterized the politics of the Kingdom of Italy from the start. Its first act, virtually on the heels of Italian unification, was the acquisition of the Bay of Assab by the Rubattino shipping company in 1869.

Zoppe's story covers the temporal arc just before the Walwal incident, or Abyssinia Crisis (1934), which served as Italy's *casus belli* against Ethiopia. Zoppe's visions also allude to some subsequent events, such as the use of poison gas (prohibited by the 1925 Geneva Protocol) during the Ethiopian War and the retaliation following the failed attempt on Rodolfo Graziani (1937). After this episode, Addis Ababa was devastated, soothsayers and storytellers targeted for persecution, accused of having incited the population to rebel against the Italian colonizers. Other instances of retaliation include the bloody massacre of the deacons at the monastery of Debra Libanos.

My research for *Adua* involved examining films, photographs, biographies of more or less famous actresses (like Dorothy Dandridge, Anna May Wong, Nina Mae McKinney and especially Marilyn Monroe), as well as studying Italian cinema (especially erotic films from the '70s - '80s) and commercial television from the '80s - '90s.

Meanwhile, Titanic comes from my work with refugees. The migrant body faces not only racism and suspicion from natives, but increasingly also distancing (or even open hostility) from the very "community" to which they belong. In the Adua-Titanic relationship there is this strong ambiguity.

For more information, I recommend the pamphlet *La negazione del soggetto migrante* (The Negation of the Migrant Subject, Stampa Alternativa, 2015) by Flore Murard-Yovanovitch.

On the subject of migrants and refugees, there are numerous books I could suggest, two of which have been essential for my own education: Nuruddin Farah's *Yesterday, Tomorrow: Voices from the Somali Diaspora* (Cassell, 2000) and Gloria Anzaldúa's *Borderlands/La Frontera: The New Mestiza* (Aunt Lute Books, 1987).

One final note; for narrative reasons, I've introduced minor anachronisms. I moved up Maria Uva's visit to Port Said by a year (it actually began in 1935) because to me this woman is symbolically important. Moreover, I have no evidence of the presence of black interpreters in Rome in 1934, though I do know, from documentary and family sources, of their presence during the Second Italo-Ethiopian War (1935 - 36). My grandfather was an interpreter under colonialism, even working for Rodolfo Graziani. For these reasons, I've always wondered about the translation process, and especially the suffering experienced by the interpreter who is also a colonial subject. I stuck to the limited and ephemeral knowledge in my possession as much as I could and the rest came from my heart and my writing.

GLOSSARY

Aabe: father
Abaayo: sister, also a female form of address
Adoon: servant, slave
Afar indhood: four eyes
Aliif, taa, miim, ra, saad, daad, shiin, siin: letters of the Arabic alphabet
Aniga waxaan ahay saaxiibka: I am your friend
Balaayo: nuisance
Bariis iskukaris: rice pilaf with meat
Beer iyo muufo: liver and muufo flatbread
Caano geel: camel milk
Cadar: perfume
Dhuhr: Islamic midday prayer
Duco: prayer, supplication
Faaliyaha: soothsayer
Gaal: infidel, foreigner, white person
Ganbar: stool
Garbasaar: shawl
Garees: woman's wrap dress
Gorgor: vulture

Gudniinka: infibulation

Guntiino: women's one-shoulder wrap dress

Hooyo: mother

Injera: bread typical of the Horn of Africa

Jeerer: nappy hair, derogatory term for the Somali Bantu

Jelabiyad: Arab-style men's tunic

Jidaal: dry season

Karbaash: whip

Labo dhegax: two stones

Macaan: sweet

Maghrib: Islamic sunset prayer

Maktuub: already written

Maskiin: poor (thing)

Munar (munaaradda): lighthouse, watchtower

Oday: old man, elder

Qofkii aammuso waa dhintay: he who is silent dies

Sanbuusi: samosa, pastry filled with meat and onions

Sanjibiil: ginger

Shaah: tea

Shaah cadees: milk tea

Shaash: head scarf

Sharmutta: prostitute

Sheeko sheeko, sheeko xariir: story, story, story of silk (the first line of many Somali folktales)

Si fiican u tirtir: dry yourself well

Siil: vagina

Tena yistilign: Amharic greeting

Tukul: hut, traditional house with thatched roof

Waan isku xaaray: I shit myself

Wallahi: Arabic oath, affirmation

Xalwo: common confection in the Horn of Africa, halva

Xayaay: help

Xus: celebration

Yaad tahay?: Who are you?

Zab: celebratory feast

ACKNOWLEDGEMENTS

I have many people to thank.

First of all, thank you to Leonardo De Franceschi. He was the person to ask me to write an afterword for his book *L'Africa in Italia. Per una controstoria postcoloniale del cinema italiano* (Africa in Italy: Towards a Postcolonial Counter-History of Italian Cinema, Aracne, 2013). That afterword led me to reflect on themes that I would later develop in this novel. Without that afterword, *Adua* might not exist. Thank you Leonardo, from the bottom of my heart.

The novel also came from another inspiration. One day the Roman writer Giacometta Limentani showed me one of her childhood photos, of her as a little girl and three probably Somali askaris in the Prati neighborhood. It was the first anniversary of the conquest of Ethiopia and Mussolini put on a big parade on Via dei Fori Imperiali. It was an incredible photo. I looked at it and my heart filled with contradictory sensations. How pretty little Giacometta was and how proud those three Somalis on foreign duty were. I also thought that those four people brought together by chance shared (even if they didn't know it at the time) a destiny. Giacometta, a Jewish girl, and the

ACKNOWLEDGEMENTS

askaris, subjects of an African colony, would go through 1938 and its atrocious racial laws. That photo in a certain sense represented the calm before the storm. This is why I included the Jewish girl and her parents in the story. The little girl isn't Giacometta, but she represents the common destiny of those who suffered under fascism.

And naturally I want to thank my family for putting up with me. Mama and Papa, first of all. Two fantastic parents who always support me. I am lucky to have such wonderful parents. Then my two brothers, Abdul and Mohamed, my cousins-sisters-more than sisters Zahra and Sofia, Ambra, Andrea, Mohamed Deq and my sister-in-law, Nura. I've been quite busy and I neglected them a little. But without them this book could not have come into existence.

I would also like to thank Rino Bianchi because in some way *Adua* grew our of our work on the book *Roma negata. Percorsi postcoloniali nella città* (Negated Rome: Postcolonial Routes through the City, Ediesse, 2014). Seeing his photographs motivated me to make *Adua* into a kind of symbol.

I want to thank my actress friends Esther Elisha and Gamey Guilavogui. Even if they are contemporary actresses, they often have to deal with a star system anchored in old stereotypes. But they are strong women and they don't give in. In a sense, *Adua* is dedicated to them, women who were able to make a destiny different than that of this book's protagonist. Esther and Gamey are fighters, and if cinema (and theater) changes in Italy it will be because of people like them.

I also want to thank Chiara Belliti, who helped me in the work of editing and taught me to trim the excess. What I learned with her will not easily be forgotten. I thank Giunti and Benedetta Centovalli for believing in this project.

And a big thanks to Shaul Bassi, Ruth Ben-Ghiat and Jama Musse Jama. This book was itinerant. I wrote it in Rome, but also in other cities, most importantly Venice (where I was Shaul's guest), New York (Ruth's), and Hargeisa (Jama's).

And I'd like to thank, in random order, the many friends who advised me and listened to me: Daniele Timpano, Elvira Frosini, Erika Manoni, Maria Cristina Olati, the "*libri in testa*" group (Elvio Cipollone, Michele Governatori, Nadia Terranova, Giuseppe Ierolli), Amin Nour, Amir Issa, Maaza Mengiste, Francesca Melandri, Katia Ippaso, Annalisa Bottani, Gabriella Kuruvilla, Viviana Gravano, Giulia Grechi, Tahar Lamri, Piergiorgio Nicolazzini, Tomaso Montanari, Tiziana Giansante, Chiara Nielsen, Frederika Randall, Clarissa Botsford, Valeria Brigida, the magazine *Internazionale*.

Enormous thanks to my Rome, muse and constant source of inspiration.

And yes, I'd like to thank Bernini. Without him, Adua wouldn't have found a big- eared elephant to tell her story to. Our cultural heritage is also an affective heritage.

Anyway, long live elephants!

If Venice Dies by Salvatore Settis

INTERNATIONALLY RENOWNED ART HISTORIAN Salvatore Settis ignites a new debate about the Pearl of the Adriatic and cultural patrimony at large. In this fiery blend of history and cultural analysis, Settis argues that "hit-and-run" visitors are turning Venice and other landmark urban settings into shopping malls and theme parks. This is a passionate plea to secure the soul of Venice, written with consummate authority, wide-ranging erudition and élan.

A Very Russian Christmas

THIS IS RUSSIAN CHRISTMAS CELEBRATED IN supreme pleasure and pain by the greatest of writers, from Dostoevsky and Tolstoy to Chekhov and Teffi. The dozen stories in this collection will satisfy every reader, and with their wit, humor, and tenderness, packed full of sentimental songs, footmen, whirling winds, solitary nights, snow drifts, and hopeful children, the collection proves that Nobody Does Christmas Like the Russians.

The Madonna of Notre Dame by Alexis Ragougneau

FIFTY THOUSAND PEOPLE JAM INTO NOTRE DAME Cathedral to celebrate the Feast of the Assumption. The next morning, a beautiful young woman clothed in white kneels at prayer in a cathedral side chapel. But when someone accidentally bumps against her, her body collapses. She has been murdered. This thrilling novel illuminates shadowy corners of the world's most famous cathedral, shedding light on good and evil with suspense, compassion and wry humor.

THE YEAR OF THE COMET
BY SERGEI LEBEDEV

A STORY OF A RUSSIAN BOYHOOD AND COMING of age as the Soviet Union is on the brink of collapse. Lebedev depicts a vast empire coming apart at the seams, transforming a very public moment into something tender and personal, and writes with stunning beauty and shattering insight about childhood and the growing consciousness of a boy in the world.

MOVING THE PALACE
BY CHARIF MAJDALANI

A YOUNG LEBANESE ADVENTURER EXPLORES THE wilds of Africa, encountering an eccentric English colonel in Sudan and enlisting in his service. In this lush chronicle of far-flung adventure, the military recruit crosses paths with a compatriot who has dismantled a sumptuous palace and is transporting it across the continent on a camel caravan. This is a captivating modern-day Odyssey in the tradition of Bruce Chatwin and Paul Theroux.

THE 6:41 TO PARIS
BY JEAN-PHILIPPE BLONDEL

CÉCILE, A STYLISH 47-YEAR-OLD, HAS SPENT THE weekend visiting her parents outside Paris. By Monday morning, she's exhausted. These trips back home are stressful and she settles into a train compartment with an empty seat beside her. But it's soon occupied by a man she recognizes as Philippe Leduc, with whom she had a passionate affair that ended in her brutal humiliation 30 years ago. In the fraught hour and a half that ensues, Cécile and Philippe hurtle towards the French capital in a psychological thriller about the pain and promise of past romance.

ON THE RUN WITH MARY
BY JONATHAN BARROW

SHINING MOMENTS OF TENDER BEAUTY PUNC-
tuate this story of a youth on the run after
escaping from an elite English boarding school.
At London's Euston Station, the narrator meets
a talking dachshund named Mary and together
they're off on escapades through posh Mayfair
streets and jaunts in a Rolls-Royce. But the
youth soon realizes that the seemingly sweet dog
is a handful; an alcoholic, nymphomaniac, drug-addicted mess who can't
stay out of pubs or off the dance floor. *On the Run with Mary* mirrors the
horrors and the joys of the terrible 20th century.

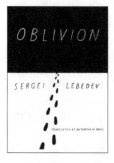

OBLIVION BY SERGEI LEBEDEV

IN ONE OF THE FIRST 21ST CENTURY RUSSIAN
novels to probe the legacy of the Soviet prison
camp system, a young man travels to the vast
wastelands of the Far North to uncover the
truth about a shadowy neighbor who saved his
life, and whom he knows only as Grandfather
II. Emerging from today's Russia, where the ills
of the past are being forcefully erased from public memory, this masterful novel represents an
epic literary attempt to rescue history from the brink of oblivion.

THE LAST WEYNFELDT
BY MARTIN SUTER

ADRIAN WEYNFELDT IS AN ART EXPERT IN AN
international auction house, a bachelor in his
mid-fifties living in a grand Zurich apartment
filled with costly paintings and antiques. Always
correct and well-mannered, he's given up on
love until one night—entirely out of character for him—Weynfeldt decides to take home
a ravishing but unaccountable young woman
and gets embroiled in an art forgery scheme that threatens his buttoned
up existence. This refined page-turner moves behind elegant bourgeois
facades into darker recesses of the heart.

THE LAST SUPPER BY KLAUS WIVEL

ALARMED BY THE OPPRESSION OF 7.5 MILLION Christians in the Middle East, journalist Klaus Wivel traveled to Iraq, Lebanon, Egypt, and the Palestinian territories to learn about their fate. He found a minority under threat of death and humiliation, desperate in the face of rising Islamic extremism and without hope their situation will improve. An unsettling account of a severely beleaguered religious group living, so it seems, on borrowed time. Wivel asks, Why have we not done more to protect these people?

GUYS LIKE ME BY DOMINIQUE FABRE

DOMINIQUE FABRE, BORN IN PARIS AND A LIFE-long resident of the city, exposes the shadowy, anonymous lives of many who inhabit the French capital. In this quiet, subdued tale, a middle-aged office worker, divorced and alienated from his only son, meets up with two childhood friends who are similarly adrift. He's looking for a second act to his mournful life, seeking the harbor of love and a true connection with his son. Set in palpably real Paris streets that feel miles away from the City of Light, a stirring novel of regret and absence, yet not without a glimmer of hope.

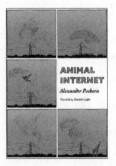

ANIMAL INTERNET
BY ALEXANDER PSCHERA

SOME 50,000 CREATURES AROUND THE GLOBE—including whales, leopards, flamingoes, bats and snails—are being equipped with digital tracking devices. The data gathered and studied by major scientific institutes about their behavior will warn us about tsunamis, earthquakes and volcanic eruptions, but also radically transform our relationship to the natural world. Contrary to pessimistic fears, author Alexander Pschera sees the Internet as creating a historic opportunity for a new dialogue between man and nature.

Killing Auntie by Andrzej Bursa

A young university student named Jurek, with no particular ambitions or talents, finds himself with nothing to do. After his doting aunt asks the young man to perform a small chore, he decides to kill her for no good reason other than, perhaps, boredom. This short comedic masterpiece combines elements of Dostoevsky, Sartre, Kafka, and Heller, coming together to produce an unforgettable tale of murder and—just maybe—redemption.

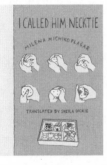

I Called Him Necktie by Milena Michiko Flašar

Twenty-year-old Taguchi Hiro has spent the last two years of his life living as a hikikomori—a shut-in who never leaves his room and has no human interaction—in his parents' home in Tokyo. As Hiro tentatively decides to reenter the world, he spends his days observing life from a park bench. Gradually he makes friends with Ohara Tetsu, a salaryman who has lost his job. The two discover in their sadness a common bond. This beautiful novel is moving, unforgettable, and full of surprises.

Who is Martha? by Marjana Gaponenko

In this rollicking novel, 96-year-old ornithologist Luka Levadski foregoes treatment for lung cancer and moves from Ukraine to Vienna to make a grand exit in a luxury suite at the Hotel Imperial. He reflects on his past while indulging in Viennese cakes and savoring music in a gilded concert hall. Levadski was born in 1914, the same year that Martha—the last of the now-extinct passenger pigeons—died. Levadski himself has an acute sense of being the last of a species. This gloriously written tale mixes piquant wit with lofty musings about life, friendship, aging and death.

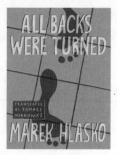

ALL BACKS WERE TURNED
BY MAREK HLASKO

TWO DESPERATE FRIENDS—ON THE EDGE OF the law—travel to the southern Israeli city of Eilat to find work. There, Dov Ben Dov, the handsome native Israeli with a reputation for causing trouble, and Israel, his sidekick, stay with Ben Dov's younger brother, Little Dov, who has enough trouble of his own. Local toughs are encroaching on Little Dov's business, and he enlists his older brother to drive them away. It doesn't help that a beautiful German widow is rooming next door. A story of passion, deception, violence, and betrayal, conveyed in hard-boiled prose reminiscent of Hammett and Chandler.

ALEXANDRIAN SUMMER
BY YITZHAK GORMEZANO GOREN

THIS IS THE STORY OF TWO JEWISH FAMILIES LIVing their frenzied last days in the doomed cosmopolitan social whirl of Alexandria just before fleeing Egypt for Israel in 1951. The conventions of the Egyptian upper-middle class are laid bare in this dazzling novel, which exposes sexual hypocrisies and portrays a vanished polyglot world of horse racing, seaside promenades and nightclubs.

COCAINE BY PITIGRILLI

PARIS IN THE 1920S—DIZZY AND DECADENT. Where a young man can make a fortune with his wits … unless he is led into temptation. Cocaine's dandified hero Tito Arnaudi invents lurid scandals and gruesome deaths, and sells these stories to the newspapers. But his own life becomes even more outrageous when he acquires three demanding mistresses. Elegant, witty and wicked, Pitigrilli's classic novel was first published in Italian in 1921 and retains its venom even today.

KILLING THE SECOND DOG
BY MAREK HLASKO

TWO DOWN-AND-OUT POLISH CON MEN LIVING in Israel in the 1950s scam an American widow visiting the country. Robert, who masterminds the scheme, and Jacob, who acts it out, are tough, desperate men, exiled from their native land and adrift in the hot, nasty underworld of Tel Aviv. Robert arranges for Jacob to run into the widow who has enough trouble with her young son to keep her occupied all day. What follows is a story of romance, deception, cruelty and shame. Hlasko's writing combines brutal realism with smoky, hard-boiled dialogue, in a bleak world where violence is the norm and love is often only an act.

FANNY VON ARNSTEIN: DAUGHTER OF THE ENLIGHTENMENT BY HILDE SPIEL

IN 1776 FANNY VON ARNSTEIN, THE DAUGHTER of the Jewish master of the royal mint in Berlin, came to Vienna as an 18-year-old bride. She married a financier to the Austro-Hungarian imperial court, and hosted an ever more splendid salon which attracted luminaries of the day. Spiel's elegantly written and carefully researched biography provides a vivid portrait of a passionate woman who advocated for the rights of Jews, and illuminates a central era in European cultural and social history.

SOME DAY BY SHEMI ZARHIN

ON THE SHORES OF ISRAEL'S SEA OF GALILEE lies the city of Tiberias, a place bursting with sexuality and longing for love. The air is saturated with smells of cooking and passion. Some Day is a gripping family saga, a sensual and emotional feast that plays out over decades. This is an enchanting tale about tragic fates that disrupt families and break our hearts. Zarhin's hypnotic writing renders a painfully delicious vision of individual lives behind Israel's larger national story.

THE MISSING YEAR OF JUAN SALVATIERRA
BY PEDRO MAIRAL

AT THE AGE OF NINE, JUAN SALVATIERRA BECAME mute following a horse riding accident. At twenty, he began secretly painting a series of canvases on which he detailed six decades of life in his village on Argentina's frontier with Uruguay. After his death, his sons return to deal with their inheritance: a shed packed with rolls over two miles long. But an essential roll is missing. A search ensues that illuminates links between art and life, with past family secrets casting their shadows on the present.

THE GOOD LIFE ELSEWHERE
BY VLADIMIR LORCHENKOV

THE VERY FUNNY—AND VERY SAD—STORY OF A group of villagers and their tragicomic efforts to emigrate from Europe's most impoverished nation to Italy for work. An Orthodox priest is deserted by his wife for an art-dealing atheist; a mechanic redesigns his tractor for travel by air and sea; and thousands of villagers take to the road on a modern-day religious crusade to make it to the Italian Promised Land. A country where 25 percent of its population works abroad, remittances make up nearly 40 percent of GDP, and alcohol consumption per capita is the world's highest – Moldova surely has its problems. But, as Lorchenkov vividly shows, it's also a country whose residents don't give up easily.

 New Vessel Press

To purchase these titles and for more information
please visit newvesselpress.com.